CLASSIFIED
Encounters

MARLO D. MAITLAND

ACKNOWLEDGEMENTS

First and foremost, I would like to thank God for blessing me with the talent and desire to be able to do this.

Thanks also goes to Bishop Bowen and The Comforting Church of Christ who, through Gods direction, steered a young man into the Air Force to make his life a beautiful adventure. Big-ups to all the people I have met along the way in my Air Force journey who inspired the characters within these pages.

Even though I have never smoked weed a day in my life, I would also like to thank Wiz Khalifa and Currensy, whose music kept my mind focused on some of the tales I was writing.

Thanks to Tananarive Due, Octavia Butler, Walter Mosley, Steven Barnes, Stephen Hunter and a slew of other writers who inspired me on this quest to be a published writer.

Thanks to my editor Fran for making me a better writer and teaching me how to 'show and not tell.' LOL.

Finally, I would like to thank my family and friends for the constant encouragement and for telling me when something I wrote was wack and pointing me in the right direction. T.Y.J.

PREFACE

T HERE ARE OVER 322 MILLION people living in the United States. There have been many debates and discussions about the one percent of the population that controls thirty-eight percent of the wealth. However, there is another, less heralded, one percent that is responsible for ensuring the safety and security of the entire United States population.

INSUBORDINATION AT 30,000 FEET

Prelude

H E TOOK OFF HIS PANTS and the *Conquistador* burst out for its grand performance. She was stunned. He smiled pretentiously when he saw her pause at the size of his conqueror. The hesitation did not surprise him because the sight of his dick made many women pause. They met two weeks before at a Bruce Bruce comedy show at the Rocker NCO club, Paul saw her before she saw him, or so he thought. Her butternut complexion and big brown eyes, which seemed to curve up at the edges, propelled a series of almost involuntary glances towards her every few minutes. She was obviously the prettiest woman in the club without a ring on her finger or a man on her arm. Paul had no intention of trying to approach her after watching a parade of men try desperately to gain her attention; she approached him instead. Sherisse Watson was her name. She was a single, Navy Chief Petty Officer and the proud mother of a ten-year-old boy named Wesley. She told Paul she had seen him working out several times at the gym and found him *interesting*. His dark, piercing eyes and thick, full lips made her pussy tingle and the thought of his hot, rock-hard body on hers made her knees buckle.

Sherisse was a sexy 37-year-old but the firmness of her body in five-inch red stilettos, skin-tight black leggings, and damn-near translucent white halter top would put some of the 19 and 20-something year-olds on America's Next Top Model to shame. Paul saw the word interesting as a double entendre, meaning she wanted to fuck him by the way she slightly licked her lips as she looked at him. He reckoned his job was to play it cool, not be an asshole, and let nature take its course. This led them to dinner at the Genghis Khan Mongolian barbecue restaurant, the living room sofa in his apartment, and Sherisse sucking and licking his balls with just the right amount of pressure that made his 9-inch dick jealous she started there first. After pausing at the sight of the *Conquistador*, Sherisse sucked Paul with enthusiasm and devotion. She deep-throated him and somehow hummed in a way that made his toes curl. It was getting difficult for him to hold on before she changed tactics and began to suck and stroke his dick with both hands, making him scream as he came harder than expected, and, to his delight, Sherisse made sure none of him was wasted.

She stood over him topless, with her jeans still on, exposing perfectly symmetrical 34Cs, and the big brown areolas that encircled her dime size nipples.

"Did you like it?" She asked with an impish grin, already knowing the answer. It took Paul a few moments to reply, still in orgasmic release as a result of her expert lip and tongue service.

"Yeah, but you already know. That was amazing! Thanks."

"That's a first. I've never been thanked before." A mischievous smile slowly spread across his face. "Come here," Paul demanded as he grabbed her waist, stood up, and kissed her harshly. He unbuttoned her jeans and slid them off. He then lifted her five-foot six one hundred thirty pound body, carried her to his bedroom, and gently laid her on his bed. He worked his mouth from her lips to her neck, all while gently circling her clit with his index finger. Paul eventually travelled to the twin peaks of perfection and laboriously used his tongue to encircle each nipple, biting them ever so delicately as to incite slight pain that translated into pleasure. He made his way down to her navel and teased her by pulling away. She moaned disappointingly and grabbed his head to push him back down, "Stop playing with me and suck my pussy, please," he smiled to himself as his ploy to have her beg for it worked. He slowly and deliberately licked her five times, then abruptly jumped up and left the room.

Sherisse was pissed until she saw him return with a big smile and a red, white, and blue *Firecracker* popsicle. He slid it in her. The initial cold of the popsicle being rubbed across her swollen clit and pussy lips shocked Sherisse at first, but the heat of his mouth right afterwards felt heavenly. Another pleasurable jolt shot through her as the coldness of the ice lolly sliding inside filled her pussy. Paul licked up the mixture of her juices and the cold confection as she squeezed her breasts in pleasure. He continued to alternate between his mouth, tongue, and popsicle until it melted. Paul made sure none of its sweetness remained between the walls of her pussy. She writhed in ecstasy as his tongue explored her inner walls and encircled her clit with licks and sucks, trying to find the rhythmic combination that would set off her orgasmic wave. Her stomach tightened and her hands grasped the back of his head as he released her pleasure. Sherisse went from holding his head in place to trying to push it away as her legs began to shake. He held her wrists while relentlessly working his tongue in the winning combination as elation reached her like an orgasmic tsunami. She screamed as she reached her peak and he felt the tension leave her body.

Paul reached between the mattress and box spring grabbing a prepositioned Magnum and rolled it on his still hard dick while Sherisse lay there in the afterglow of her orgasm. He kissed her as his knees opened her legs for entry and gently slid the *Conquistador* into her sugar walls. Sherisse underestimated the depth of Paul's dick as her breathing increased. She thought she could handle it, but she couldn't. Sherisse tried to slide away from him. He knew she was going to be a runner at that point, a disappointment. Paul tried to take it slow in order to acclimate her to his length and girth, but somehow she wound up sideways against the headboard whenever he got into a groove. Tired of chasing her around, he pulled her gruffly to the edge of the king-sized bed, turned her over, and entered her from the back with her legs pinned against the bed so she could not escape. Paul began his strokes long and slow at first; however, the intensity of his rhythm increased as he became more aroused. The force of his thrusts made her beg for mercy. She tried to weasel out from under him while simultaneously pulling the sheets off the bed in an effort to gain traction for her escape.

Paul had no mercy for Sherisse. He made tears come to her eyes with the pain and pleasure of his wrecking ball-like thrusts. Her legs began to shake and tremble again. She attempted to push him off of her even as she started to have another orgasm. Trapped in a beautiful conundrum of pain and pleasure, she screamed again as Paul felt her pussy squeeze his dick and undulate with the pressure of another orgasmic tsunami. Her guttural screams into the pile of bed sheets and the grip of her pussy as she came excited him. He felt his climax come from deep within his testicles and his voice joined hers in a cacophony of bliss. He collapsed on her as she came again with only the spasms from his throbbing dick. "You're a mean son-of-a-bitch, you know?"

"You didn't like it?" Paul inquired, feigning innocence.

"No," she smirked, "I always scream at the top of my lungs when I have a bad time." Sherisse put her clothes on while Paul watched. He smiled with bravado as he noticed the change in her walk caused by the *Conquistador*.

"I'll be doing remedial Kegel exercises for a month because of you," she grinned.

Paul just smiled while inwardly glowing with pride over his dick size and ability.

"I'll give you a call later, okay? I need to get my little man from my girlfriend's house."

"Okay, make sure you let me know when you made it home safe," Paul replied.

"I'll do that." She kissed him goodbye and called him

thirty minutes later at 2345 to let him know she was home soaking her sore vagina in a warm bath. He was asleep by 2355, only to be awakened at 0300 by a call from work.

#

Technical Sergeant Paul Cana, or *Flaco*, as his family and friends affectionately called him, was a crew chief on KC-135 airplanes in the United States Air Force. KC-135s refuel other planes in mid-air; however, they are also used for medical evacuations and moving cargo on occasion. In emergencies, the aircraft is used to transport service members and their families to certain military or civilian locations to receive medical care otherwise unavailable at their current location. It was on such a mission that Flaco now found himself, along with his assistant and fellow crew chief, Senior Airman Bobby Lee Chismowsky, or '*Ski*' as he was called due to the constant butchering of his last name. Ski was a hefty 5'8" white guy from Montgomery, Alabama who loved his fair share of domestic beer, country music, chewing tobacco, and loose women, in that order. He was a good ole' boy in every sense of the word. Flaco, on the other hand, was a 6'1" slim, olive-skinned Puerto Rican from Camden, New Jersey. While the contrast and difference between the two of them was startling, they were comrades in every way and they looked out for each other like brothers.

Flaco was called and alerted to the mission at 0300 on a Saturday morning, which gave him an hour before he had to report in at the plane and be ready to go. Alert crews, like medical doctors on call, as well as the maintenance personnel who fly with them, like Flaco and Ski, are not supposed to drink any alcohol. They need to be airborne within two to three hours after notification. Flaco did not drink at all, so he had no issues. Ski, however, was out gallivanting with friends until 0200 in the morning, finding it impossible to be in a bar and not have at least 5-6 beers. When they got the alert, Ski immediately called Flaco to let him know he had fucked up.

Shit! I have to pick up Ski's country ass on the way to the plane. There's no way he can drive his drunk ass in, Flaco fumed in thought as he grabbed his bag before leaving his apartment.

"What the hell is up man? You know we're on alert. I know you like to drink every day, but can't you just hold off for 72 fucking hours?" Flaco berated Ski.

"I know TSgt. Cana, I'm sorry 'bout this, but I got caught up at the going-away bash for T.J. Not to mention a redhead with the biggest tits this side of the Pacific! HUAAH!" Ski exulted.

"Yeah, yeah. I know how you dudes get around a source of alcohol and fast women," Flaco retorted. "The only reason I am not turning you in right now is because this is our third alert mission and you never did this shit before." His ire now cooled, he returned to his normal tone of voice and said, "Try to keep your ass downwind of the flight crew, and remind me to grab that Polo cologne out of my locker when we get to work so you can spruce yourself up."

Sensing the anger gone out of his cohort, Ski went back to informal terms.

"Flaco you know I use nothing but Irish Spring and Right Guard," Ski complained.

"You gonna use some new shit today. Once we get out

there and start sweating, whatever you've been drinking is going to start coming out your pores; and, for both our sakes, I'd rather have you smell like Polo than beer, Jack Daniels, or whatever else you been drinking."

Ski remained quiet. He hoped the medical crew smelled nothing suspicious on him when they got there. He also prayed that the plane got off the ground without incident, so he could get to the crew chief bunks in the back of the plane, crawl in his sleeping bag and go to sleep. They arrived at aircraft 58-6969 at 0355 before the fliers or the nurses showed up and started getting the plane ready for flight.

"I smell like a madam in a Chinese whorehouse with this shit you sprayed on me," Ski sniffed his shirt, snorting in disgust.

"Better that than catching a charge for being drunk on duty, and having money taken out of your pocket because you lost a stripe!"

"Whatever Flaco. I still don't like this shit!" Ski nagged.

"Stop whining, fat boy, you might smell good enough to get one of those nurses or flight medics to notice your hefty ass," Flaco laughed.

"Have you seen the movie *Full Metal Jacket*?" Ski asked.

"Of course man! That's a classic!"

"Well, this is prime Alabama white snake," Ski motioned to his genitals, "And I don't need this skunk shit sprayed all over me to get a girl." They both enjoyed a hearty laugh at Ski's comments before the pilots showed up to give them a brief on the mission for the day. To Ski's dismay, it was going to be a long one. They were scheduled to fly from Kadena Airbase in Okinawa, Japan to Andersen Airbase in Guam to pick up a mental patient and then fly him to Hickam Air Force Base in Hawaii, where he could get specialized care.

When the medical crew arrived, they were briefed again on the specifics and condition of the patient they were to pick up. It turns out that the patient, Nate Gordon, was labeled *homicidal* by the medical crew. Furthermore, he threatened to kill his wife and supervisor for fucking around while he was on a temporary duty assignment to Korea for 30 days. Since Mr. Gordon, a civilian employee of the government, agreed to behave on the flight, he was not strapped down. It turned out to be a mistake. While the patient was not deemed violent, the crew was asked to keep an eye out for any strange behavior in case of an emergency. It was during the briefing that Flaco got a chance to examine the medical crew he was flying with. It consisted of two female officers, both nurses, and two medical techs, male and female, who were enlisted. The nurses were Captain Faye Dunham, a white woman in her late forties, and First Lieutenant Felicia Grant, a gorgeous woman with a smooth, chocolate complexion. She reminded Flaco of N'bushe Wright from the movie *Dead Presidents*. He normally let Ski listen to the briefings while he readied the plane for take-off, but this time he let Ski do all the work and he listened to the brief by Lt. Grant. He tried to convince himself that he was doing this because he did not want anyone to smell Ski. However, the truth was he wanted to get a better look at the lieutenant.

After her briefing, Capt. Dunham pulled her aside and appeared to point out some things that she may have missed or should have included in her brief. Although she was paying attention to Capt. Dunham, she couldn't help but look in Flaco's direction. Her smile revealed a deep dimple in her left cheek and her pearl white teeth looked so good in contrast to her dark smooth skin. He watched as she put lip-gloss on and noticed the beautiful shape of her now prettier, shinier lips. He delighted in her sensual mannerisms and was lured into her muse. He quickly returned the smile and went back to doing his job as he felt an involuntary warmth growing in his loins. *It's really hard to hide a hard-on in a flight suit*, he thought to himself, as he struggled to stop imagining the color of his olive-toned hands in contrast gripping the Lt.'s naked chocolate ass from behind.

With his mind now focused and with Ski's assistance, Flaco helped the nurses and techs load up their equipment and place it around the patient support pallet, or PSPs, as they were called. PSPs are put on the KC-135 to accommodate medical passengers. All the crewmembers worked in unison to set up the equipment so they could take off on time. Lt. Grant held Flaco's gaze as they carried out their respective duties. He felt the hairs on his body rise as if electrified whenever she got close to him while they worked together. Even her brown hair bundled in a classic chignon allured him. He was glad that flight suits were unflattering to the female physique, because a hard dick would not do him any favors right now. *Too bad she is an officer*, he thought, as he mused on the rules governing fraternization and the illegalities of the enlisted-officer relationship.

Once the medical crew was finished loading the 35 x 10-foot cargo area of the KC-135, they were finally able to close the door and get the engines started. They took off at 0515 and had a three-hour flight to Guam, with a six-hour flight to Hawaii. The PSP's were set up near the front of the cargo area near the lavatory and cockpit. The crew chiefs normally sat near the rear of the cargo area during takeoffs and landings, and then climbed to their bunks above the boom pod area on the right side of the airplane. Just a few feet forward of the boom pod area on the left side of the cargo compartment, was a box that contained two auxiliary power units or APU's used to start the engines. Forward of the APU's were two wooden bins used to keep luggage as well as aircraft equipment. If someone stepped down into the boom area on the left side no one could see them from the front of the plane.

The flight to Guam was uneventful. While they loaded the psych patient with no undue events, Flaco had a funny feeling about the guy and told Ski he did not like the looks of him.

Ski grinned in a macabre manner, "You city folk are too paranoid sometimes. *They* said he was 'crazy' not craaazzzy." Flaco just ignored his partner while looking at the man the nurses referred to as *Mr. Gordon*.

Mr. Gordon was possibly an inch or so taller and definitely heavier by at least 30-40 lbs. Flaco could not gauge his age, but assumed Mr. Gordon to be several years older than him, he was in fact only 2 years older than the 27 year old Flaco. However, mental issues and forays into depression had aged his features considerably. The medics said Mr. Gordon was safe, Flaco wondered how homicidal and safe wound up in the same sentence. The threats to his wife and supervisor had only been verbal, and there were no physical actions to go with them to consider him dangerous to anyone but the two people who betrayed him, so his mental state was deemed safe. Flaco watched him like a hawk for the first 45 minutes after takeoff, until he dozed off not knowing Lt. Grant was looking at him admirably from her side of the airplane.

Unbeknownst to him, Flaco was very much appreciated by Lt. Grant. The 5'8" chocolate stunner was attracted to men she could still put heels on with and not feel like their mom. The University of Southern California graduate, or USC as most notably known, from Los Angeles, California was very liberal in her taste of men, and had enjoyed dalliances with a myriad of hues during her undergraduate years in college. The patch on his flight suit labeled Boricua made her wonder if what some of her girlfriends told her about Puerto Rican men enjoying eating pussy was true. She had been with a few Mexican men who loved to fuck and eat pussy as much as any other man, but this type of Spanish man alerted her senses. She smiled to herself and her thoughts wandered to how different her flavors of love have been, but she never had a Puerto Rican before.

Mr. Gordon stood up suddenly, the strange look on his face breaking the Lieutenant out of her reverie. They were now an hour and fifteen minutes into their flight to Hickam and Mr. Gordon's face alone alarmed her. Capt. Dunham approached him and asked him to sit down and relax when all hell broke loose.

"YOU DID THIS TO ME!" He screamed and pushed Capt. Dunham into one of the med techs while moving towards the cockpit where the two pilots and the boom operator, who was in charge of controlling the boom during refuel operations, were located.

He means to kill us all! Lt. Grant thought, terrified at what was unfolding in front of her. The boom operator left the cockpit to investigate the screams of the nurses and headed towards the cargo compartment. He was met by Mr. Gordon and was dealt two crushing blows to the face that had him dazed on his feet. At this point Flaco was awakened by the screams and commotion. He immediately ran to the front of the cargo area past the screaming medical personnel just in time to stop Mr. Gordon from landing his third blow on the boom operator that would have surely left him unconscious. Flaco grabbed Gordon's right arm and spun him around forcefully knocking him into the lavatory door, "What the fuck are you doing?"

Mr. Gordon, surprised momentarily by the turn of events, only paused for a few seconds before focusing on Flaco and directing his aggression towards him. "YOU DID THIS TO ME!" He lunged at Flaco. The boom operator struggled to regain consciousness and composure from the near fatal blows while Flaco bore the brunt of his madness.

"Ski!" Flaco yelled desperately as Mr Gordon rushed at him. Unfortunately, Ski's beer-induced sleep kept him oblivious to the fact that a paranoid schizophrenic was trying to crash the plane and kill them all. The slim Boricua was outweighed by 30 lbs of mass but the avid cross-fitter was stronger than his frame belied. Flaco could dead lift 400lbs, squat 325lbs, and had recently got a new one-rep max at bench press of 310lbs. Those statistics do not matter with a well-timed punch to the jaw; however, it was a factor as Mr. Gordon grappled with Flaco and slammed him into the opposite side of the aircraft. Instincts from street fights as a teen in Camden kicked in as the southpaw struck two rapid fire blows and dazed Mr. Gordon enough to gain his release. He put Mr. Gordon in a sleeper hold and squeezed, holding on for dear life.

Flaco was strong, but he knew he had to try to end the fight quickly because the type of aggression Mr. Gordon had would not bear well for him in a prolonged skirmish. Flaco held on to the larger mans neck while being clawed and slammed against the PSP's and walls of the plane until the deprivation of oxygen to the brain caused Mr. Gordon to lose consciousness. The fracas had taken maybe three minutes from start to finish but it seemed like an hour. The nurses and techs were stunned as Flaco stood over the unconscious man breathing heavily.

"He will only be out for a little bit. I didn't kill him so if you have something to keep him from doing this again, I suggest you give it to him now."

Spurred to action by Flaco's words and the moaning of Mr. Gordon, Capt. Dunham told Lt. Grant to grab their bag while she checked Gordon's vitals. Satisfied with the result and that he would not die due to his brief strangulation, she injected him with a sedative that would keep him under for the rest of the flight to Hawaii. Dazed, the boom operator leaned against the lavatory door assuring the now present co-pilot that everything was okay.

Flaco was not without visible damage. The left side of his face was scratched badly, and his back was also heavily bruised. The Captain, although still visibly shaken, took charge of the Lt. and two med techs to lift the now drugged patient on to a litter of the PSPs and strapped him down. Once he was secure, they began tending to Flaco, who had now retreated to his earlier place near the rear of the airplane. As the adrenaline rush of the fight wore off, Flaco suddenly felt a wave of exhaustion that coincided with the burning sensation from the scratches on his face and the serious throbbing pains in his back. Lt. Grant was still feeling the trepidation about what had just happened, even though the danger was now over.

Flaco could see that her demeanor had changed since everything had taken place, and he tried to make a joke out of it when she and the tech came near to treat him.

"Don't be alarmed Lt., I normally choke someone out on every flight. As you can see, my partner over there didn't even budge." He smiled nodding towards the sleeping and now snoring Ski in the top bunk. Lt. Grant and the female tech laughed and, just like that, Flaco saw the beautiful woman he gained appreciation for back at the briefing on Okinawa.

"Are you okay? Let us know where you have any pain." Up close she was even more stunning and beautiful than he imagined. Her complexion was dark chocolate and smooth, with no blemishes that he could see. Flaco felt that familiar warmth in his loins again. *Fuck! I don't need this shit right now!* He forced himself to clear his mind of wanton thoughts of ravaging the young lieutenant, who was about to treat his injuries.

"My back hurts pretty bad right now," he winced from

whatever solution the tech was using to treat the cuts and scratches on his face.

"You're going to have to take your shirt off so I can see your back." He was glad that he chose to wear some underwear under his flight suit on that day. On occasion, due to the heat and high humidity on Okinawa during the summers, he would refrain from wearing anything but a t-shirt; but today he was safely clad in some Calvin Klein boxer briefs. As he raised his shirt over his head, the Lt. saw his muscled stomach and her mind began to wander to places not fit for proper nurse-patient relationship or officer-enlisted relationship for that matter. The moisture in her pussy increased tenfold while prodding and feeling his muscled back for broken bones. *Shit! Even his fucking back is sexy!* She was sorry to hurt him while she examined his back, causing him to shift uncomfortably as she touched him. A deep bruise had already formed where he had been slammed against the fuselage and the PSPs, but the feel of his skin and the heat emanating from his body excited her. She was glad that she forgot to follow protocol and put on latex gloves even as she attempted to have a softer touch.

It took every bit of self-control Flaco possessed not to get a hard on while she examined him, as her hands against his skin left a lasting impression. He still felt her hands at the previous location as if his back was wet concrete and she was making handprints all in it. It felt great.

"You don't have any broken bones, but those are some serious bruises back there. Motrin or Naproxen will help you with the pain."

"Thanks Lt. I appreciate it. I could use one or two of the M-vitamins," Flaco joked in reference to the Motrin. She smiled and the dimple appeared again.

"No! Thank you. We may be in the ocean right now if not for you doing what you did, you know, saving us and all. I am just sorry you got hurt in the process. Those scratches on your face should heal without scarring, by the way."

Lt. Grant looked him over once again to make sure they did not miss anything before beginning to repack the kit they were using.

"Did you guys know that dude could go psycho like that?" Flaco asked.

"Hell no! I mean, no Sergeant, we did not. He was supposed to be non-violent."

"Well, I am glad it's over and he's out and strapped up. Maybe I can join my snoring friend in dreamland."

"Go ahead, you deserve it after all this. What Capt. Dunham gave him will keep him out until we get to Hawaii." Lt. Grant passed him two pills of Motrin. Flaco grabbed his water and took the pills in one gulp and watched Lt. Grant return to her seat. She could still feel the muscles in Flaco's back and the heat from his body. She wished she could have felt his abs and slid her hands a little lower to see if his dick was hotter than the rest of his body. *I need to stop thinking about that motherfucker*, she felt her wetness saturate her undies and went to the bathroom. *I wonder what he would do with this pussy if he knew it was so wet for him.* She used a wet nap to wipe her pussy and tried to air out her undies wishing she thought to bring panty-liners. *Hmph, he couldn't handle this*, she thought to herself with utmost confidence.

Flaco was spent. The fight and the struggle of keeping his body in check while the Lt. examined him had tired him out. He walked up to the cockpit to check on the boom operator and the pilots, and to get a timeline on when they would be landing. Amazingly, they still had another 4 hours before they would arrive in Hawaii.

Damn! Flaco felt like they had been flying for ten hours already. He was looking forward to being on the ground again so he could get into a real bed as opposed to his sleeping bag in a bunk in the back of the airplane. The pilots and the boomer thanked him for subduing the psycho and he returned to his bunk intent on trying to get some sleep and imagine the feel of Lt. Grant's hands on parts of him that were not bruised. They exchanged smiles as he passed by and she watched him remove his boots, and slide into his sleeping bag.

Capt. Dunham had tended to the boomer with unsteady hands. The experience for her was the closest she had ever knowingly come to death. With her adrenaline high, she soon crashed after calm was restored. She did not realize her wrist was sprained until she finally sat down, after assuring the pilots the patient was under control and sedated. Lt. Grant wrapped her wrist, gave her a little Motrin, and the Captain suddenly felt exhausted and knew she would not be able to function without some type of rest.

"Listen Grant, this is way out of regulation, but my eyes are closing on their own. I need a power nap for at least an hour. After all this shit my nerves are shot. Can you handle it?"

"I'm fine Capt. He won't be waking up anyway."

"Ok, wake me up in an hour. No more, no less okay?"

"I got you, Capt. Dunham. I will set my alarm for an hour from now." With that said, Capt. Dunham leaned back and was enveloped in a deep sleep almost immediately.

Lt. Grant sat in her seat replaying everything that happened that day and was proud that she felt so calm in spite of it. She was as scared as everyone during the melee, maybe even more so, considering it was her first mission, but at that very moment she felt great and happy to be alive. Her thoughts suddenly returned to TSgt. Cana, and how he made her feel at ease with just a few words when she was still in a scared daze. She replayed his heroic acts in her mind over and over again. He was like a live action hero who jumped out of nowhere, ready to subdue the crazy ass man they picked up from Guam.

Here we go again. Her pussy swelled and began to rapidly moisten once more. *Fuck this! I almost died, and if I want to fuck a fine ass Puerto Rican that just saved my life I will.* She decided to take matters into her own hands so after assuring that Capt. Dunham was asleep and the med techs were occupied with watching the comatose Mr. Gordon, she headed to the back of the airplane.

She walked with nervous excitement, as she was about to turn thought into reality. She knelt down next to the bottom bunk with the sleeping TSgt and slid her hands into his sleeping bag. She slowly zipped his flight suit down so she could feel what she had thought about since she first laid eyes on him. She could hear and feel her heart beating excitedly over the noise of the engines. Surprisingly, as she slid her hands against his abdomen under his boxers, she found his member already hard. When her hand circled his hot hard dick his breathing pattern changed. She did not want him to jump up excitedly, so with her right hand still holding his dick, she put her left hand on his chest, leaned into his ear, and whispered "Hey, it's Lt. Grant. I just wanted to give you a proper thank you for saving my life."

Flaco's eyes opened with a startled look and made motion to get up, but she held him down.

"Shhh! Let me do this. Don't move." She felt him relax and his dick flexed in her hand as she made her way down to his mid-section, extracting his dick from his flight suit and boxers, so she could circle his engorged head with her mouth.

Flaco inhaled sharply as she used both hands in circular motions with her mouth in tandem to perform her ministerial duties. Flaco was ready to explode sooner than he wanted to. He tried to slow her down by pushing her off of him, but she slapped his hand away and continued without missing a stroke. He could see her cheeks move inward as she sucked his dick with extreme pressure. Resistance was futile, as he felt the insatiable wave rise from his toes to the head of his cock. When he climaxed in her mouth, she continued sucking and using both hands more urgently moaning as well as if she was tasting a unique delicacy. She licked the tip of his still hard dick before moving back to whisper in his ear, "Thanks for not being insubordinate and allowing me to thank you properly." She licked his ear lobe and got off her knees to head back to her station. Flaco grabbed her wrist, stopping her while rising in one motion to push her behind the APUs. He kissed her while zipping her flight suit down to explore the body within. Discovering a voluptuous ass that felt perfect in his hands, he squeezed it fiercely.

He reached under her t-shirt pulling her bra straps through and lifted her shirt from her waist in one smooth move to access her hardened nipple with his hot tongue. She grabbed the back of his head as she felt him inhale sharply over a nipple and cool it before putting his hot mouth back on it. Her senses were reeling as she felt herself being lifted up while he stepped down into the boom pod area. His fingers inadvertently slipped into her wet pussy as he tried to carefully bring her down to taste her, and she moaned with pleasure. Placing her gently down in front of him with her flight suit tangled around her ankles, he licked his fingers before kneeling to pull her panties to the side. He ran his tongue from the base of her pussy to her clit and stayed there while she moaned in ecstasy. *His mouth is so fucking hot!* She tried to open her legs wider to feel more of him but was thwarted by the flight suit around her ankles.

"Wait!" She whispered harshly as she hurriedly unzipped one leg of her flight suit to pull it out, so he could have full access to her core with his mouth and tongue. She moaned, as he continued sucking while circling her clit with his tongue. As she leaned up against the APU with Flaco expertly working his tongue and mouth between sucking and licking her clit, she found herself covering her mouth to stifle the scream she wanted to let out as she neared orgasm. The APU prevented her from backing up from the urgency of his mouth. She tried to angle her hips down to remove herself before she screamed and woke the snoring crew chief on the top bunk. Flaco just slid his hands under her now entirely slick ass and lifted her torso off the ground, while he continued to suck on her until she had to use both hands to stifle the noises she made as her body shook uncontrollably with her climax. He gently let her hips down and grabbed her behind her back and stood up so he could explore her mouth once again with his tongue.

She kissed him before pushing him away to say, "I heard Puerto Rican men could eat pussy, but damn!"

"That's not all we can do," He whispered, as he maneuvered her past him into the boom pod on her knees so he could enter her from behind. She was glad the area was padded as her nails dug into the cushion while his length and girth slid into her very wet center. They both closed their eyes as his full 9 inches disappeared inside her. Initially, Flaco just stilled himself and made his shaft flex inside her while she pushed herself back into him to get it deeper. Her movements both surprised and excited him because he was used to women running from the initial feel of his size but she met him head on so he matched his thrusts with hers as she reached behind herself with one arm to grab his ass and pull him in deeper. He leaned over her and whispered, "You need more?" Her eyes said it all when she glanced over her shoulder at him and licked her lips lasciviously. Flaco's thrusts became more urgent as he decided to give her a good pounding. Lt. Grant met him full bore at first, but one of those deep strokes hit her in a spot that made her lie down while stifling an involuntary scream.

She could see the sky out the boom window and could not believe she was fucking above the clouds. Flaco was still giving it to her as she lay on her front, enjoying the view and the thorough fucking she was getting, when she felt his rhythm change to staccato, a sign that he was going to come again. Lt. Grant started to pump her hips in rapid-fire fashion while reaching back again grabbing his ass to keep him inside her as she heard his muffled moans through gritted teeth. She felt his exploding excitement as he continued assaulting her pussy until she buried her face into the cushion and screamed, coming again soon after he did. Flaco sat on the boom steps admiring Lt. Grant's ass as she slowly rose from her laying position.

"That boy can sleep, can't he?" She nodded at the still snoring Ski while getting dressed.

"Yeah I guess so," Flaco laughed.

Once she was dressed the Lieutenant leaned into the still seated TSgt. Cana and kissed him before saying "Thanks again for saving my life and taking all the stress out of me when I was still scared and unsure of my job earlier." "You are welcome," was all he could say as he moved out of her way allowing her to return to her seat next to Capt. Dunham. Flaco lay back in his bunk in a dream like state in disbelief of what just happened and dozed off. Hours later a tap from the boom operator awakened him to let him know they were on final approach and needed to get strapped in their seats for landing.

The plane landed in Hawaii without incident. Flaco watched as Lt. Grant and the rest of the medical crew loaded the still unconscious Mr. Gordon into the ambulance. They left the airfield as he and Ski did their checks in order to leave the plane and head to the hotel. While putting on the engine covers Ski finally noticed the scratches on Flaco's face.

"What the fuck happened to you? You look like you had a fight with Wolverine," a genuine concern in his voice. The irony of everything that happened during the past few hours and Ski's obliviousness to it all made Flaco drop his end of the engine cover and roar with laughter. The dumb look on Ski's face at his response made him laugh even harder as he finally said between fits of laughter,

"Ask me in a few years, you sleepy ass Rip Van Winkle motherfucker!"

DESERT DESSERT

I WOKE UP ALL OF A sudden at 5 o'clock in the morning with another two hours to go before I had to be at work. The time of my abrupt awakening pissed me off for two reasons. First, I could *still* be sleeping during the best part of sleep. Second, I was having a wet dream about Damien, my sometimes fuck buddy back in San Diego. Shit! I wasn't in love by any means, we were just casual lovers. Damien had a big, hard dick and juicy lips that sucked my pussy and licked my ass like nobody's business. I suppose I subconsciously needed the real thing after six plus months of playing with myself out here in Iraq. My pussy was still throbbing from the fading dream of Damien's affection, so I licked my fingers and closed my eyes while I circled my clit slowly, trying to remember what his mouth felt like in the dream.

My moans were loud and boisterous. I couldn't help it and I didn't care who was around. My former roommate, a Navy chick, had just redeployed back to Norfolk, Virginia and I was finally all alone, but who knew how long that would last. I gasped, as I felt the intensity of my orgasm explode while climaxing to Damien's memory. I knew I would make the head of his succulent dick swell immensely if he knew I got off to him like this. *Hmmm… maybe I should send him an email to tell him. Fuck that! I am going to Skype-fuck him! He would love that.* I licked my fingers enjoying the sweet and salty taste of myself, wishing I was licking my pussy juices and cum off of Damien's chin after having my goods eaten so expertly. "Damn! I could use a real live partner right now," I said aloud to the empty room.

I sat up in my single bed with the clock now reading 0545, fifteen minutes before I normally got up to walk over to the showers before work. Without a roommate I didn't have to fumble around in semi-darkness with a flashlight or pen light trying not to wake her up, so I turned on the bright, fluorescent lights. I looked at myself in the little mirror inside my open wall locker and enjoyed the sight of my deep cinnamon-colored skin against the pale cream of my *Secret Vickies*. My roommate found it weird that I would wear such extravagant items, but I hated feeling like a robot every day. Being deployed in a war zone as a Marine, my two wardrobe choices were Camos and PT uniforms, not a plethora of options by any means. So I ordered a few color-inspired satin and translucent mesh lingerie pieces from some of my favorite sexy, female apparel boutiques. I need to feel like a woman and not a machine. And believe it or not, I actually miss wearing heels, the higher, the better. I especially like the ones that strap around my ankles and lower legs. Damien practically came in his pants from the sight of me in stilettos, and I loved getting that kind of a reaction out of him. After a long night at the club, I could not wait to get out of my 5 and half inch heels. However, right now

I would love to put on a red hot pair and strut my stuff. My body is to die for now too, and I can't even show off the way I want. Hell, I will probably have to get a whole new shoe collection soon due to my feet spreading from wearing these damn combat boots and sneakers every day.

I took off my cream-colored undies and put on my PT gear while grabbing my toiletries and towel for my cool morning shower. I was glad our brave guys outside the wire and the unmanned drones disposed of the fools who used to send mortars and rockets at us in flurries every morning. Now I don't have to wear a flak vest and helmet just to go to the showers. I enjoyed the hot, rising sun as I walked to the shower billets while simultaneously being annoyed by the loud F-16s taking off, although I was more than used to it. The Air Force boys are a little soft, but I love what they do. The warm breeze passing through my legs sans panties felt like a sensuous caress as it sent an erotic chill up my spine. I closed my eyes for a moment and shook my head, "I need some dick!" I said out loud drowned by the roar of the jet engines. The cold shower barely helped my still stimulated libido. I was glad once again not to have a roommate so I didn't have to be mindful of the noise I made getting dressed. I checked my hair to make sure my braids were not frizzy from the desert heat. I may have to redo it in a few days. I said my prayers and read Psalm 91. I did that every day while I was out here as my grandmother asked me to. She, Granma Lulu, found out I would be out here in potential danger and made me promise to keep this routine. I threw my cover on, took one last glance at myself before pouting my pretty pink lips together, and blew a kiss at my reflection while heading out the door to my office at the hospital.

My name is Renita King, Staff Sergeant Renita King, to be exact, but everyone calls me 'Nita. I am a proud Marine or *Devil Dog*, if you know the lingo. I serve as a liaison between the injured Marines coming in from the forward operating bases and their families at permanent duty stations, while I am deployed in Iraq at Balad Airbase. I get soldiers phone cards and other comfort items while they are transitioning from here to Ramstein, Germany or back to "The States" if the injuries merit it. I sometimes have to make calls to distraught family members if the Marines are unable to speak for themselves due to injury. My job is hard and demanding, even draining at times, but job satisfaction is also phenomenal. Although I don't like being here, I love my job and I know I am making a difference in someone's life every day. The only thing missing is a glass... make that bottle of good wine or cranberry juice with two shots of Pineapple Ciroc and a good dicking-down after work to ease the tension of a hard day.

The men outnumber the women here in *The Sandbox* and the variety is limitless, as well as the degree of *fineness if you will.* However, the risk of disappointment makes me hesitant to chance losing rank for some non-discreet lame that could not fuck or eat pussy if his life depended on it. I made that mistake when I first got here with an Army Sergeant who from the outside, especially outside his pants, was one of the finest men I had ever seen. We flirted a few weeks before he was scheduled to go back to Ft. Campbell in Kentucky, so I figured I could take a chance since I would never see his ass again. He was such a good-looking motherfucker! I have a weakness for pretty boys. What a mistake! First of all, in a war zone most military members are not allowed to be in the quarters of someone of the opposite sex as part of General Order 1. So, as an alternative, he had to sneak me into his room since I had a roommate at the time and I did not know her well enough to ask for a little space. I couldn't imagine going up to her asking, "Hey girl, do you mind leaving the room for a few hours so I can smuggle some dick in?" Not happening! Anyway, we cloak and daggered my ass into his room. The excitement and anticipation from all the weeks of flirting and sneaking around to get here had my pussy so fat, fatter than what it already was. Little did I know what I was getting myself into.

We had kissed a couple of times before I decided I would fuck him. He kissed very well, which I normally took as a good omen to other bedroom proclivities, so I felt I was in good hands. I never grabbed his dick in our make-out sessions, choosing instead to focus and feel on his arms and chest. Big mistake! Too bad he could not fuck me with those parts of his body. I had never been fisted before but I seriously contemplated asking this guy to be my first after the bullshit I went through. Anyway, I am in his room and my t-shirt and bra are off almost before the door is fully closed. He awkwardly slobbers my 36 D's when I grabbed his dick through his shorts. I knew I had fucked up. His dick was smaller than what I imagined a 12-year-old kid would have! After he came, before he even fucked me, I might add. I found myself hoping he could eat pussy and saying it to myself over and over again while clicking my heels in my head as if I was Dorothy in The Wizard of Oz. Needless to say, my mantra went unanswered. I serviced myself when I got home after experiencing the most disappointing sexual episode of my life; however, that only takes you so far. I practically swore off sex in the desert after that disappointing experience.

A few butch or stud girls approached me alongside the guys, but why would I fuck with a woman? Especially one who looks harder than any dude I would ever fuck with. It seemed like the girls who fashioned themselves like men were sometimes more aggressive than the guys. Like Waka Flocka, those motherfuckers go hard in the paint. I like dick, make no mistake about it. Being with another woman... nonsense, if you ask me. I mean, I appreciate another good-looking woman although I never crossed that line. I will be damned, though, if I allow another woman to get near my goods regardless of how good she says she would eat my pussy. I don't know how some of these chicks do it with other women like that. A woman can't do anything for me sexually. Or so I thought.

The long, hot days blended together out here in this arid place. Even though mortars and rockets are less frequent, they still come daily. I was walking out my door on my way to the gym when I saw her, effortlessly walking into the pod next to mine. She was light-skinned with medium, green hazel eyes and lips a lighter shade of pink than mine. She wore tight jeans, a t-shirt, and wheat colored Timberland field boots completed her ensemble, which reminded me of those East Coast girls I met after I joined the military. Her ass was also amazingly big. It was really very nice, if I do say so myself. I could already see the looks she would receive at the dining facility or anywhere around the base she chose to go. I consider myself a "bad bitch," but my new neighbor was definitely beautiful in anyone's vocabulary. Damn! Did I mention the size of her ass and how good it looks? I decided right then and there to do extra squats and lunges to tighten up, although I feared I would never achieve her level of ass "greatness" without major surgery, or these new ass shots I keep hearing about.

My new neighbor's name was Saphira Honeycutt, and as I suspected she was an East Coast girl, from Philadelphia to be exact. Saphira was a civilian contractor working for Kellogg, Brown, & Root, hence the tight jeans and Timberland boots. Our first conversation was about my hair. She stopped me on my way to the gym one day and asked me who braided my hair.

"Oooh girl, your hair is always so pretty. It looks so healthy. Who braids it?"

"I do it myself about every two weeks since I can't wear it down out here, and I go to the gym almost every day so I try to keep it out the way. This dry, desert heat is murder on my hair," I replied.

"I can tell already. Look at my ends," she grabbed her blondish hair to show me.

"I would do it more often, but the water here is so hard. I know it's damaging my hair, but that's another story."

"Well, I wish I had long, pretty, auburn hair like yours," Saphira said as she genuinely admired my hair. I told her I would hook her up if she needed it and we became cool after that. I was also pleasantly surprised to know that she enjoyed the game of chess as much as I did; it was great to find a woman who knew the game and could actually play.

While braiding Saphira's long, soft, honey-blonde hair on yet another long, hot ass day, I found out she was a vegetarian as well. How she managed to have an ass like that without eating any meat still amazes me to this day. My cool Chicago mannerisms amused her, especially when I shared my story of disgust and disappointment with that lame-fuck-ass Army Sergeant.

"I don't mean to disparage the whole Army because I am sure there are more than a few well-hung cock-slingers serving our country well, but unfortunately for me I chose the wrong one." Saphira laughed so hard she was wiping tears from her eyes. "Well, I never had that problem," she chuckled again. I soon found out why. About a week after I braided her hair, we bumped into each other at the showers. I was coming in from the gym and she was drying herself and putting her clothes on to head back to her room. "Hi 'Nita!"

"Hey girl!" I tried, unsuccessfully, not to look at her naked ass too hard while she dried herself. Her breasts were not as big as mine, but her ass more than made up for it. Plus, I am sure you could find about a hundred guys or more in a two-mile radius that would co-sign my sentiment.

"Are you off tomorrow?" Saphira asked while she continued to dry herself.

"Yeah, I finally get to sleep in and decompress after six twelve-hour days at the hospital."

"I just got the first three seasons of "The Game" from

the Iraqi's at the little bazaar if you want to come over and watch it after you take your shower," Saphira said while pulling her shirt over her head.

"I just might do that since I have a roommate again. I was going to go over to the recreation center or library but I'll stop by."

"I'm the only female here with my team, so you can chill out in the extra bed. I got a box of snacks and goodies from my brother in the mail that you're welcome to share as well."

"Thanks! I will definitely come through after I wash my ass." I took off my PT gear and got in the shower.

Saphira answered her door in a pair of navy blue boy shorts that barely maintained full coverage of her ass cheeks and a tight, light blue t-shirt that showed off her perky little B-cups. I love my body and I am confident as all get out, but I always wanted a bigger ass, so my 36Ds made me feel pretty good when compared to Saphira. Her room smelled sweet like a combination of ripe mangoes, golden peaches, and assorted berries. The sheen on her body parts revealed that it was not just air freshener that smelled so sweet as I glanced over and saw a who knows what of lotions and oils in her wall locker. She did not have a roommate, nor would she ever have one, so her pod was set up a little differently than mine. Where the wall lockers in my room were in the middle of the room with the beds to either side to give the semblance of privacy, her lockers were off to one side; I could see she had separated the single beds so I could have one to myself. She sat on her bed eating a bottle of Maraschino cherries her brother sent her. It was her favorite snack. We sat in her room laughing and bullshitting watching "The Game" and eating cherries when I realized Saphira's eyes were roaming over my body and lingering on my breasts. Her look was a little different than I was used to from a woman and, truthfully, it made me a little nervous.

"Do you want some water?" She asked as she got up and walked over to her little fridge. Another luxury I did not have.

"Sure, I'll take one." I admired the way the shorts had rode up on her ass exposing more cheek than I thought humanly possible without wearing a thong. I tried pushing the thought of Saphira being both pretty and sexy out of my head. I was already chastising myself for my fascination with her ass. I was curious to see how it felt, and embarrassed I felt that way at the same time. *Shit! Lack of dick and this desert air must have my brain screwed up*, I thought to myself. I sat there stewing in my own thoughts for a few minutes when I glanced over at Saphira and locked eyes with her. She was playing with a cherry stem in her mouth. Damn! She is fucking sexy! She stood up smiling and moved to my side of the bed leaving an empty space between the two beds, "Nita, can you get up for a second please?" I was a little apprehensive about being close to her, so I got up on the opposite side from her in between the two beds. "You're going to have to get from in between there so I can do what I've been wanting to do since I met you."

"Okay," I said a little timid and suddenly unsure of myself as I moved out the way. She pushed the two beds together and then, somehow, I found myself tasting the cherries on her tongue while her hands cupped my face.

She then slid her hands down my shoulders and arms to reach under my shirt and deftly unsnapped my bra.

I offered no resistance. I suddenly wondered if I was a lesbian, but at that moment I didn't care. Our tongues danced so well together that I left the thought behind me and enjoyed the moment. She lifted my shirt over my head and sucked on one of my breasts while squeezing the other one perfectly. My pussy was suddenly wetter than it's ever been. I don't know if it was because this was something new or she was just that good, but it felt like her hands and mouth were all over me and we were still standing up.

"You are so beautiful; you know?" She whispered against my ear as she turned me around and kissed the back of my neck. Her kisses cascaded my spine with her tongue moving my shorts and panties off in one fell swoop to start sucking on my ass cheeks and playing with my clit at the same time. I moaned aloud as my clit was expertly maneuvered by this obvious grandmaster.

"You like it don't you?" She ran her nails lightly down my leg, making me shiver.

A heavy moan was all I could muster as she came back up my spine, still handling my clit to perfection. I felt myself coming close to an orgasm, so I pushed her hand away to gather my wits. Damn she was good! I turned around to see her sucking my delight off her fingers.

"'Nita, your pussy is so tasty. Come here let me show you," she said before kissing me passionately again. I tasted just as good in her mouth as I did in Damien's, maybe better. As our tongues tangoed, I grabbed her ass finally and it felt good. I squeezed it while we kissed and heard her moan in response. I was glad she liked it. I know I did. I took her shorts off and then her tight top before we moved into the bed. My skin felt like it was on fire with everything she did to me. I was getting off by seeing how she responded to what I was doing to her even though we were just feeling and kissing each other. I was glad that the TV was on because I already knew that when I climaxed it was going to be loud and uncontrollable. It seemed like we kissed and fondled each other for hours before I worked my way down to her little Bs. I engulfed them in my mouth one at a time and softly played with her nipples between my teeth. I watched her stomach flutter when I moved down to her clit and began to draw the alphabet with my tongue as Damien sometimes did.

"Uhh huh! Yeah!" She grabbed the back of my head and held it in place tenderly. "Come here," she whispered harshly. She maneuvered me into position so we could eat each other's pussy. Her tongue moved so fast on my clit that I couldn't do her in a proper fashion. She tapped my ass and pushed me forward.

"Come up here and feed me that pussy," she demanded, as she turned me around and pulled me up so I could sit on her face.

"Fuck!" I yelled as she stuck her tongue deep inside me. She then sucked on my clit while somehow simultaneously rolling her tongue across it. I held on to the headboard as she checkmated me into a climax. "Ahhh, Saphira, right there! RIGHT THERE! OH YEAH! OH YEAH! OH YEAH! YES! YES!" I screamed as my first orgasm hit me like a Mack truck. She stuck her finger in my ass midway through my orgasm and I felt another climax come up unexpectedly.

"Oh shit you bi…" I stopped mid-sentence because the feeling was so intense, but she held on torturing me with pleasure until I had to throw myself to the side of her in order to escape. I shuddered as the climax shockwaves of my second orgasm had my body shaking without my control.

She had captured my queen and definitely the fucking king. Her fingers traced my body as I continued to shudder. Checkmate indeed. I needed to get her off me because I was so sensitive. I grabbed her hands and began to kiss her again as I worked my way down to her clit to see if I could win my re-match. I pushed her legs back with my forearms like Damien would do. When I licked her ass, she tried to force her legs down as she moaned with pleasure. Check. I was glad her thighs were not super big and that I worked out, or I would have lost the battle right there. I went back to her clit and sucked it while tweaking it between lips and tongue. Saphira continued to show me a high approval rating by moaning more heavily. I licked her asshole again, and her body jolted in such a fierce way that I almost lost control of one of her legs.

"Oooh…do that again," she breathed.

"Turn over first," She did as I asked, and I began to suck and lick those ass cheeks until I finally decided to spread them and give her what she wanted. She cocked her ass up to allow me proper access to her soaking, wet pussy and eager ass. Her legs began to shake almost immediately as my tongue darted around and in her rear hole. She grabbed a pillow and screamed into it loudly while she came. Mate.

I wondered if all girls with big asses had a set of extra nerves in their ass that allowed them to orgasm like that since it had never happened to me before.

"Damn, 'Nita, that was good."

"Shit, you were good too," I replied as we continued to share small kisses.

"I better be since I don't fuck with men." Essentially letting me know women were her preference. I suppose the realization that I had just slept with a woman for the first time showed up like a neon sign shining across my face.

She smiled assuringly, "Don't worry 'Nita, I can tell this ain't your thing, but you took to it like a fish to water."

"Blame it on the heat and those damn cherries," I said, as we both laughed. We fell asleep kissing and caressing each other intertwined like snakes. I woke up in the morning to feel Saphira sucking on one of my nipples before she headed out the door to take a shower. I went back to my room to see my new roommate getting ready to head out.

"Where have you been SSgt King?" she asked.

I just smiled back and said, "Don't ask, don't tell…"

WEAPONS OF MASS DESTRUCTION

THE SHOOTING THAT TOOK PLACE last week had Delano shaken up. Antonio and his street pharmacy fraternity had recently tried to shoot some rivals unsuccessfully. They failed to eliminate the competition, so retaliation was in order, and Delano almost lost his life in the crossfire. He was not even involved with any of the drug dealing war parties. Although Delano was not a drug dealer, he was known to hang out late at night on the bench during peak crack sale hours with his cousin, Antonio, who worked for Kelvin and his gang. On that particular Friday, he was just in the wrong place at the wrong time. The near death experience got him thinking about how to get the fuck out of New York. The recent high school graduate and attendee of Kingsborough Community College in Brooklyn was bullshitting with his life. After attending Kingsborough for a year, he only had 9 credits instead of 24. The failures were not due to any lack of intelligence, just laziness and youthful foolishness, like waking up at the last minute, only to decide against going to class. He abandoned an opportunity to attend Berkeley University in California, simply because he did not want to take the SAT exam. Instead of taking advantage of a once in a lifetime opportunity, he chose to go to a junior college for two years with plans of attending a four-year university afterwards. But life has a way of altering plans. Delano was young, gifted, and foolish. So now the projects were getting hot, and because of family ties and affiliations he almost got shot. He needed a change of scenery before the volatile situation placed him in a *kill or be killed* situation.

Delano remembered the last time he went down to The Junction, a lively, cultural, and small business Mecca at the intersection of Flatbush and Nostrand Avenues, and saw a line of military recruiting offices. He decided to inquire about what they had to offer. On his way there, he mused about how stupid he was for not taking the SAT in order to go to UC Berkeley. He thought he had all the time in the world to do whatever he wanted to do in life. *I'd probably be in Cali right now*, he thought. All the offices were lined up together: Army, Air Force, Coast Guard, Navy and Marines. It was like the government bought out a little piece of the block. Only in Brooklyn would you see the recruiting offices right next to the Jamaican restaurant selling beef patties, the Vietnamese nail salons, the African street vendors selling knock-off designer bags, the Muslims selling fresh bean-pies, and all that.

As Delano slowly walked toward the Army recruiting office, he suddenly stopped. He found himself entering the door to the Air Force recruiting office instead, as if in a trance. He saw a gorgeous woman in a sky blue top with four stripes on the sleeve inside. At the time he had no idea what the stripes meant, but later on he discovered she was a Staff Sergeant, E-5, in the Air Force. She had cinnamon colored skin and her hair was cut in a bob that accentuated the roundness of her face. It was then that he decided he wanted to join the Air Force, and he was glad he did. There were actually two women in the office, but he did not see the other one until he went in.

The smiling woman that made him do an about face out of his Army platoon dreams said in a very professional manner, "May we help you?"

Suddenly short of breath Delano tremulously replied, "Yeah, um, what do I have to do to join the Air Force?" She stood up from behind her desk and offered him the seat on the opposite side. She was not big in the hips, nor did she have one of those asses so big that you could see it from the front; but, she did have a big, beautiful pair of breasts with nipples erect and very visible through her sky-blue uniform top.

Maybe it's the chill from air conditioning that's making those tits pop, he thought. Her intense eyes and inviting smile further seduced him to have a seat. Delano considered that, given the opportunity, he would go after that pussy as if he was President Bush looking for weapons of mass destruction.

"Hi I'm Staff Sergeant Leblanc and that is my office partner Sergeant So & So." She did not actually say *so and so*, but that is the only thing Delano heard as he tried to refocus his thoughts on what he really came into the office for and not the beautiful woman in front of him. He was in the office for about 30 to 45 minutes, answering and asking questions about the entry process. SSgt. Leblanc told him he needed to take a practice

ASVAB test before taking the real one for entry. As he walked in a back room of the Air Force office, he noticed two high school looking desks and a couch sitting across from a long wall mirror that was probably there for them to check themselves out. Delano did exceptionally well on the practice ASVAB test, so SSgt. Leblanc set him up for the real thing to include his physical and everything. He was proud of his decision to join the Air Force at his age because many of the people he grew up with were on a fast track to nowhere. That was his frame of mind four weeks after that first day in the office, as he got ready to leave for the Military Entrance Processing Station in Fort Hamilton, Brooklyn under the Verrazano Bridge. SSgt Leblanc did him a favor by picking him up and driving him, even though he could have easily taken the train. She shook his hand and wished him good luck on the test and physical. He liked the feel of her soft hand in his, and held on to it a little longer than necessary thanking her for all her help. Two weeks after going through the test and physical he had an appointment to meet SSgt Leblanc in her office at 5:30 p.m. to get the results back. He wondered why she asked him to come so late, especially when they closed at 6:00 p.m.

He arrived 20 minutes after 5 o'clock. SSgt. Leblanc had a client in front of her.

"Hi Delano!" she smiled. "Have a seat there at my partner's desk and I will be right with you."

He liked the way she said his name. In fact, he wondered how she would sound with his thick, nutty, caramel delight all in her. He smiled mischievously to himself as she dealt with her recruit. Twenty minutes passed slowly while he waited for her to finish signing a skinny, bigheaded Puerto Rican kid. When he finally left the office, she locked the door, closed the blinds, and changed the open sign to closed. He noticed how nice her ass fit into the tight, Air Force blue skirt of her uniform.

"My office partner is on leave right now and I am going home after we are done, so I don't need any interruptions." She tapped the chair opposite of hers, ushering him into the seat as she went to the file cabinet for his paperwork. She was aroused by Delano's smooth caramel-colored skin and his chiseled physique. It was quite obvious that he worked-out on a regular basis. His body displayed the result of push-ups, pull-ups, and dips in the project park. His deep, dark eyes, pearly white teeth, and juicy lips further enticed her. He was sexy, handsome as fuck, and she wanted him.

"Well, sir, your tests look pretty good. You passed the written test with flying colors, so you can basically pick whatever job you want, provided it is available. And," pausing to shift his file around, "your physical was good also. I see here you don't have AIDS, a great thing, and your cholesterol levels are good as well. You seem to be in top notch physical and mental condition," SSgt. Leblanc smiled deviously.

"I'm glad that I'm good on all levels," Delano smiled back in response to SSgt. Leblanc's jovial nature. "So, what else do I have to do?"

"Ahhh, we have one more thing to accomplish," another devilish smile appeared as she got up from behind her desk. "Follow me," she ordered as she walked in front of him going into the back room.

He stared at her little backside and admired its petite nature. She had a nice curvature that appealed to his eyes. SSgt. Leblanc suddenly turned around and caught him looking down at her ass. She smiled appreciatively while Delano tried to look anywhere but her face.

"You have one more test to pass." She grabbed both of his hands and pulled him close, placing his hands on her ass. She tiptoed a bit and kissed him passionately. The stiffness and shock at her actions turned into electric relaxation as she sucked softly on his bottom lip.

"Mmmm...I love juicy lips," she whispered in between sucking and kissing. She let his hands go and reached between his legs feeling the growing bulge in his pants. He was instantly hardened for duty. SSgt. Leblanc no longer had to tip toe because he was very much involved and proactive in the exchange as he turned the tide and licked and sucked on her lips. She moaned while caressing his muscular, sculpted chest.

"You can kiss! Your tongue is teasing me. What else can you do?" She asked.

"Let's find out," he reached her lower back in an attempt to undress her. Sergeant Leblanc took a step back and began to slowly unbutton her sky blue top. Her nipples were at full attention. The Leo in Delano took a step forward ready to pounce on his prey, but he was stopped by her shaking head.

"Just watch," she said with authority. His thick dick throbbed as he enjoyed the sight of the sexy, brown vixen undressing in front of him. He began to undress himself while keeping an eagle eye on SSgt Leblanc.

"I told you to watch! If you are going to join the military, you need to learn to follow orders," she commanded with a smile. His dick jumped and stiffened as he was not used to being told what to do, but he did it nonetheless. With her shirt and bra off, he saw that he was not wrong about the beauty under her clothes. His mouth watered a little and he almost laughed at the irony of feeling like a little kid wanting to suck on some breasts but he kept himself in check. No room for giggling like a schoolgirl, while grown-folk's business was happening right in front of him.

"Do you like my girlfriends?" She stroked her breasts and clutched her nipples harshly.

"Yes, I do!" He watched her sucking on her own nipples, "Let me show you."

"No way! Your orders are to watch until I say otherwise." He continued his vigil as she undid her skirt and dropped it to the floor. She then teasingly removed her copper-colored boy shorts. His dick got harder as he looked at her naked in front of him.

"Now you can move. Move Airman!" She ordered. They began to kiss and tongue duel again. He enjoyed the feel of her breasts in his hands as she unhooked his belt and undid his pants. As soon as his jeans fell to the floor, she pulled his Tokyo Laundry boxers off. She held him back again as she examined his missile. She ran a few fingers along his thick shaft and with the tip of a finger took the moisture from the head and licked it.

"Mmmm, have you been eating a lot of pineapples lately? Tastes sweet." He did not speak a word but his third leg jumped in response. She saw the spasm and laughed while grabbing his hand to lead him to the couch.

She sat him down and then got on her knees in front of him, appraising his dick as she held it.

"I like the curve in it," she took him in her mouth to begin her homage. As her warm, wet mouth covered his head, he closed his eyes and let a moan escape his lips, letting her know that her mouth had the correct moisture levels. She moaned too as she diligently sucked on his dick. He opened his eyes to their reflection in the mirror. It excited him to see her naked and dutifully working on him through the mirror, but what excited him more was seeing the juice from her pussy slowly fall down her legs while she took care of him. Her cascading moisture reminded him of a commercial where they poured honey into a cereal bowl. The excitement of pleasing him stimulated her too. She was astounded by how thick his dick was. *Damn, he's fine,* she thought as she spat on his dick and tried to do her best impersonation of Karrine Stefans AKA 'Superhead.' He felt his cock stiffen so much it almost hurt as she slurped and sucked his dick with a loud enthusiasm. He grabbed her hands, hoping to stop her before he came into her mouth, but she continued. He smiled remembering a verse from Jadakiss about getting wireless head as he finally understood what the rapper meant. He had to gently extract himself from her mouth while easing her head back with both of his hands.

"Am I too much for you?" She looked at him before licking off the dollop of sweet cream that had formed on the tip of his dick he had been unable to withhold.

"We will see who is talking shit in a minute Sergeant." He lifted her off her knees and placed her next to him on the couch.

He knelt down in front of her and nodded at the wet spot on the floor. While tracing the stream down her inner thigh, he asked, "What's that?"

"It's like that sometimes." As she shrugged her shoulders and smiled in what he saw as a challenge, he smiled and roughly snatched her hips and legs up while putting his mouth on her clit.

"Yeah, Airman!" She moaned, as he circled the nerve center with his tongue. He sucked on her nub while pinning her legs up in the air with his hands to keep her fully open. She tried to get away from his mouth and the movement of his tantalizing tongue. He countered this by putting his arms under her legs and grabbing her waist to lock her in place, continuing his work. Her legs began to shake as he continued to suck on her succulent pussy, then he felt her stiffen, shudder, and lock up while desperately trying to get him off of her.

"Ahh, ahh...st-...st-...stop! Sh-...sh-...shit! Shit! Shit!" She struggled to shout while her legs stiffened up as if she had rigor mortis. He let her go and stood her up only to fold her over the edge and back of the couch. He plunged his juicy dick in her fat pussy from behind. The groans were in sync this time, as they joined together and felt each other's warmth.

"Oh shit!" He yelled as he felt her tight cunt clutch his cock.

"You love this pussy, don't you Airman?" He pushed a little deeper and made her moan to close her mouth.

"I know you love it!" He ignored her taunts and continued fucking her, while playing with her clitoris until she started trying to get away from him again. He tightened his grip on her little hips digging deeper as her legs and body began to stiffen of their own volition. She had tears in her eyes when he let her go and she slid down the couch unable to stand as she continued to enjoy yet another orgasm.

She had a smile, along with a look of awe and satisfaction, on her face, "I have never come more than once before in such a short span."

"I am not done yet, Ms," he grabbed and stroked his still swollen member as he stared at her with a fierce desire.

She sat up on the couch and patted the spot next to her, "Let me see if I can put that good thing down," Delano did what the SSgt wanted. SSgt Leblanc climbed on top of him and lowered herself to sheath his dick with her pussy, it was her favorite position. She sucked on his lips as she gyrated to the beat of her own internal drum. *Damn!* He thought as he felt her riding him expertly. He grabbed her ass and felt the sweat and slickness there. He took the middle finger of his right hand and gently slid it into her ass as she continued to ride him. She threw her head back and grinded on him even harder. Her pussy was gushing so much it sounded like a malfunctioning washing machine in the room.

"Oh fuck! Ooooh...I'm coming again!" She moaned.

"Don't stop baby, I am right here with you!" She fucked him harder as they came simultaneously. She loved the feel of his hot load inside of her. He was so sensitive he tried to push her off after he came but she grabbed him tight around the neck and kept moving.

"Now you know what it feels like," she whispered in his ear while continuing to grind on him. He just sat still and absorbed the chills running throughout his body. Once she finally unsheathed him he noticed her wobbly legs as she stood up and sat down in one motion. He smiled with a sense of accomplishment.

SSgt Leblanc smiled back, "You passed the final test with flying colors! My goodness!" After they got dressed, SSgt Leblanc gave him the basic training start date and told him what to expect as well as what he needed to prepare for. He showed gratitude for all the help and she thanked him for the lovely evening. It was nine o' clock and the street outside was still alive and jumping when they walked out of the recruiting office. The sound of Bob Marley's Pimpers Paradise coming out of the Jamaican restaurant dominated the air.

SSgt. Leblanc drove Delano back to the projects and kissed him before he exited the car saying, "Maybe we will find those weapons of mass destruction, after all, with good men like you on the job."

He laughed recalling the thoughts of his first day in the office, "I think I already have."

BRINKSMANSHIP

Brooklyn Kital, or BK, as called by her peers in Flight A of the 1st Special Operations Security Forces Squadron, was getting ready to start her new job as an aide/secretary for the Command Chief of the base. After a little over four years as a cop, with three deployments under her belt, she was ready to leave the Flight and get away from her career field.

She had been promoted to Senior Airman 'Below The Zone,' a reward which allows those selected to get promoted six months early. She also made Staff Sergeant on the first attempt, proving her hard work and intelligence to be an asset to everyone. She reluctantly admitted to her supervisor the desire to cross-train out of Security Forces or separate from the Air Force altogether. Realizing that she needed a break from being a cop, and wanting to keep a good Non Commissioned Officer in the career field, her supervisor Technical Sergeant Dexter Karger talked to his superior to see what he could do about it. TSgt Karger wanted to get her the time to re-evaluate her thoughts on whether she really wanted out of the Air Force or not.

The Flight Chief, Master Sergeant Myrick, put her in for the Command Chief's secretary position so that she could see the Air Force from a different perspective. MSgt Myrick understood what TSgt Karger saw and wanted to try and keep an obviously smart and talented young person in his Air Force.

26-year-old Brooklyn was from Milwaukee, Wisconsin. She left the state to escape the cold winters, and the colder presence of her mother, who never seemed to be happy about anything. After graduating high school she contemplated going to college even though she didn't want to go back to studying, especially without a good source of income. Her mother couldn't afford to send her to school and her father was a non-factor in her life, so college was put on the backburner.

Deciding to enter the Air Force, after seeing some recruiters in uniform at a supermarket one day, was a no-brainer. When she arrived at the Florida panhandle, she knew somebody upstairs was looking out for her because the place looked exquisite. Coming from the cold and bleak of Wisconsin, she felt the dark veil of her city and home being lifted off as the plane landed.

Engrossed in fervor, she learned the job and applied a trait instilled in her by the elder Ms. Kital, work as hard as you can and be the best you can, wherever you find yourself.

She enjoyed the dorm life and the white sand beaches amongst her friends when she wasn't deployed, but the times between deployments were few and far between. One of the added benefits of becoming a Staff Sergeant was that she would be forced to get out of the dorms and into her first apartment, an endeavor she was excited about and looking forward to.

She was due to move out within the week, which would put an end to one of her favorite late night pastimes, visits from the *Night Eater*.

TSgt Mikhail Rodgers was the Section Chief of Flight B and had been one of her trainers when she first arrived in Florida at Hurlburt Field. However, their last deployment added a new dynamic to their working relationship, leading her to leave her dorm room open at least once a week, so she could get a visit from TSgt Rodgers. The *Night Eater* would come in to her room where the bottomless, or naked, BK would awaken to his hot tongue licking between her thighs until she woke up. She enjoyed it so much because she could not reach climax by any other means and he never asked her to do anything. She would just lay back and enjoy being pleasured until he released her tension with his mouth, sometimes even twice. They were both committed to not being committed, so this worked in everyone's favor. He enjoyed pleasing her, and what red-blooded American woman would not enjoy getting her pussy eaten without expectations? It was akin to having a living sex toy.

He came in around 0130hrs and locked the door behind him. She was asleep and did not hear him as usual. It was early June in Fort Walton Beach and the temperature had been above 95 degrees so Brooklyn slept naked due to the central air in the building being on the fritz. He stood there for a moment, enjoying her nakedness and her deep dark chocolate skin enveloping her 5'7" frame. Smiling, Rodgers washed his hands before getting ready to handle the delicate parts of her body and walked over to her.

She was a hard sleeper and didn't flinch when he gently pulled her to the edge of the full-size bed, adjusted his weapon and radio, and got on his knees to spread her pussy lips with his tongue. His strokes were long and languorous, starting from the bottom and pausing at her clit to flick it a few times before going back to the starting point. Never losing contact with the pink center of the chocolate he was dining on, he felt her juices starting to flow. The wetness on his chin increased as he stuck his long tongue as deeply as he could inside her pussy. She then moaned deep and awakened, reaching down to caress his head. She tossed his beret to the side and spread her legs wider while gently pulling on his ears to get his tongue deeper. He pressed it on the roof of her sex eliciting another moan and another attempt to get his tongue deeper and deeper.

"Damn Night Eater," she came twice with the long strokes of his tongue as her moans and the sound of his radio filled the room.

The next three weeks saw Brooklyn furnish and decorate her new apartment while getting on the job training from SSgt Raquel Cepeda, the previous NCO in the position she was taking over. Command Chief Master Sergeant Bert Monds was her immediate boss and supervisor, but they both worked for the Commander, Colonel Carl Texeira, a man she had yet to meet.

The Wing was having a 4th of July weekend barbecue bash for the military members and their families, so everyone was expected to attend. Mandatory fun was in order! After four weeks on the job, Brooklyn knew that as a member of the Commanders Support Staff she could not miss the event, so she made her way to Okaloosa Island.

She pulled up to the beach area parking lot and saw a group of men, young kids, and teens playing volleyball in the sand, and her eyes were immediately drawn to the dirty-penny colored, tall, bald man who looked like he modeled for the Insanity workout commercials. Walking up to the benches alongside the volleyball court, she saw the Commander's civilian secretary Mrs. Masako and sat down next to her.

"Hey Mrs. Masako," Brooklyn smiled.

"Hey girl, how are you today?"

"Hot," Brooklyn laughed.

"I know that's right girl. This Florida heat is serious," she laughed too. Brooklyn paused, taking off her sunglasses to clean them. "One thing that is cool out here is looking at that tall brown man over there. Definite eye candy for women and probably some men too nowadays," she giggled.

"Young girl, you do know that's your Commander, right?" Mrs. Masako laughed.

"Stop lying Mrs. Masako!" She jumped up in surprise to look at her.

"I forgot that you never met him," Mrs. Masako grinned. "You don't look at the pictures on the wall you pass every morning either, I take it?" She asked.

Brooklyn just stood there with an incredulous look on her face and Mrs. Masako burst out in laughter again when Brooklyn sat back down next to her with that look still plastered on her face.

Colonel Texeira's parents were from Trinidad but his

mother was of Indian descent and his father was black, so the blend of ethnicities gave him a unique bronze complexion. Brooklyn was intrigued and shocked at the same time, his abs were something out of the Muscle and Fitness magazine much less his chest and arms. Mrs. Masako tapped her on the knee, breaking her out of that train of thought.

"Are you going to say something, Brooklyn?" mirth still in her voice.

"I'm sorry Mrs. Masako, but you messed my head up with that one."

"I understand you, girl," Mrs. Masako declared understandingly. "Colonel Tee had me wondering if something was wrong with me when I first met him. He is seven years older than me and my husband, but looks and moves like he is ten years younger. I'm still wondering what kind of special lotion he puts on his skin, or what type of secret concoction he drinks to keep him looking that way. I love my husband to death and would never step out on him, but I'm sure I would find new depths of love if he looked like that." They both laughed hysterically at that one.

She and Mrs. Masako spent the afternoon talking and laughing, with Brooklyn strategically avoiding the opportunity to be introduced to the Commander in civvies due to fear of ogling his body even more up close. She told Mrs. Masako she would wait until everyone was in uniform so her thought process would be more professional. She left the beach that day thinking it might be hard to work in the office.

Colonel Texeira was a widower who had lost his wife

to ovarian cancer ten years earlier. Upon losing his wife of 14 years, he remained a single dad raising his son, Carl Junior, on his own, minus the times he deployed when he had his mother come take care of Junior in his absence. Seeing his wife pass at an early age inspired him to take his health very seriously and he became a workout fanatic. In his home country he ate freely, cheating on his self-imposed restrictions enjoying the roti, callaloo, and everything else he grew up eating. However, in layman's terms, he was a clean eater who stayed as far away from processed foods as possible. You could often find him working out with the Para-rescue and Combat Controllers, giving them a run for their money.

Combat Controllers and Para-rescue are the Air Force's version of the Navy Seals and, although less heralded in the public eye, no less tough or dangerous. Their workouts were usually an intense combination of lifting weights, calisthenics, running and swimming, very much akin to CrossFit. Colonel Texeira often beat men younger than him in many of the timed workouts the special operators did. Needless to say, he was extremely fit and his body reflected it. The care he had for himself coupled with good genetics made him appear to be in his late 20's or early 30's as opposed to almost being 60.

Physically, Colonel Texeira was the antithesis of what she thought a Commander should look like. Something Brooklyn defined as old, stodgy, and white in her very limited Air Force career. She knew he was older than her by probably more than twenty years, but he didn't look his age at all. Rodgers worked out and had a good body, but he might as well fold up his tent if you stood him next to the Colonel.

After the long holiday weekend, she met Colonel Texeira, who was not as intimidating as she thought he would be. The Colonel's slight Trinidadian accent added an extra sexiness factor to him because she was never exposed to any West Indians in Wisconsin. As the months passed, her fascination with the Colonel dwindled down to a silent inner appreciation when he walked by. She often wondered if he was aware of her mental machinations and infatuation with fucking him.

One Saturday evening, Brooklyn went into work to make sure a memo she had to write was done to perfection, and saw the Colonel's Porsche Panamera in the parking lot. Admiring the sleek styling of the German luxury car, she thought *Even this motherfucker's car is sexy*. "His dick has to be small," she giggled to herself out loud before regaining her composure and entered the building.

Walking by his open door, she poked her head in on the way to her desk, "Hey Colonel Tee, working overtime?"

"Unfortunately it's always overtime for me, SSgt Kital, but I love it though. I get paid for this, which is a fortunate blessing."

"Payment is always good, Col. Tee," they both chuckled. "Let me go make sure this memo for the Chief is good to go Sir. Enjoy the rest of your evening."

"You too, Sgt. Kital"

Brooklyn worked on the memo for about two hours, and it was now 2130, but she was still a little unsure about the work she had done. Knowing the Colonel was still in his office, due to the green IM icon on her computer, she sent him an instant message asking if he could take a look at the memo. *Email it to me and come down to the office* popped up on her screen. Brooklyn logged off her computer and headed down to the office.

"Thanks for doing this for me, Sir."

"No problem, SSgt Kital, give me another minute to finish reading it."

As she stood on the other side of his desk, the scent of his cologne seemed to lightly waft into her nose and she felt a familiar tingle as her pussy began to moisturize itself. *Shit! I hate this sexy old motherfucker. I'm going to have to text the Night Eater as soon as I leave and hope he's free.*

The Colonel looked up, "Everything is good except for a slight format issue. Come on this side so I can show you what I'm doing, this way you know for next time."

She almost refused when he said that, but she couldn't admit she was scared to get any closer to him for fear of what her body was doing involuntarily. "OK Sir," she said while trying to psych herself out of the natural attraction with the thoughts she had before entering the building. She stood behind him, leaning forward, as he showed her what she had done wrong and how to fix it, while the scent of his Bond #9 Wall Street cologne intoxicated her.

The cologne, mixed with his man musk, caused her to go temporarily insane and without hesitation she licked his baldhead. He stopped mid-sentence, his hand frozen on the mouse. She backed away from the Colonel into the wall behind his desk, scared and shocked at what she had done and the potential repercussions to her career. After what seemed like an endless pause, he got up and walked to the door of his office, gently closing and locking it. She stood against the wall, unmoving and silent, as he walked towards her. She suddenly felt like she was swimming, while bleeding, in shark-infested waters without a knife and no help in sight.

He stood on the other side of his desk while removing the heavy leather belt from his khaki shorts and asked her, "So, you did wan' fuck me huh?" his Trinidadian accent so heavy. She said nothing, but her pussy continued to make loud exultations under her clothes. With the belt still in his hand, he called her to him and she obeyed. He pulled on the drawstring of her sweatpants while she stood in front of him, mesmerized. He slid his hand in her pants while bending down to slide his tongue in her mouth, finding both areas to be equally wet and warm.

He backed away from her and sucked the fingers that had previously been inside her. "Hmm, so you did want to fuck me," stating a fact.

This time, she found her voice, "Yes, Sir."

He smiled and began to unbutton his shorts, now displaying a considerable bulge. As his shorts dropped, she stood surprised that he had no underwear on and was awed of the thickness and length of his dick, the biggest she had seen outside a TV screen.

She was brusquely turned around while being bent over the broad, honey oak desk. Her panties and sweats came off in one motion as he stepped on her wet boy shorts and sweats to free her ankles, so he could spread her over his desk. Still gripping the leather belt in his left hand, he grabbed his dick with the right and rubbed his engorged head on her wet pussy lips ten times before sliding the full length into her pussy very slowly.

She inhaled and exhaled as his dick filled her womb better than any prior lover had ever done.

"Ahh fuck!" She whimpered.

"You like this dick," Colonel Texeira barked with authority.

"Yes, yes," she gripped the edge of the desk.

"I don't believe you like it enough so you are going to have to prove it to me or get punished. Understand?"

Brooklyn filled with his cock was at a loss for words until she felt it being removed with lightning quickness. She felt the leather belt flash across her ass and his dick thrust back in her with such force that her scream got cut short and she started to cough a little bit.

"Do you understand?" She heard through a daze.

"Yes," she responded swiftly this time.

"Good."

She felt her juices rolling down her leg so freely she felt like a slip and slide, but it was just an unprecedented level of arousal that caused her pussy to salivate. He started to give her steady rhythmic strokes as Brooklyn laid face first over his honey oak table looking like dark chocolate spread over a golden piece of toast. Every time he pushed himself inside her, he would pause for a second and pump his dick so she could feel it swell. He did this for a few minutes to the sound of Brooklyn's moans until suddenly he ripped his dick from her pussy walls to lash her three times. He continued to use his shaft as a rapid force pile driver whilst she screamed and whimpered, trying to find something to hold onto as he pounded out her pussy walls while alternately lashing her.

After pulling his dick out swiftly once again, she expected another lash but instead she felt his hand grip her hair and pull her up from the table. He turned her around, still gripping her hair, and licked both her lips before biting and giving her bottom lip a light pinch. He guided her to her knees in front of him and told her to suck his balls.

She tasted the familiar sweet salt of her own pussy and found herself suck a little harder on one of his balls, causing him a burst of pain.

"Ahhhhh! Yes, gal!" he said in his now raspier Trinidadian accent, which made him sexier to her. He guided her to his strong dick and let her show him what she could do with it.

She moistened his shaft thoroughly before licking the pre-cursor of his inevitable explosion from the tip of his dick. She submerged half of his dick in her mouth while squeezing his balls hard with one hand, and stroking the rest of dick with the other.

"Raass!" he exclaimed, as her synchronized sucking and squeezing brought him unbridled pleasure. *These young girls must go to school for this shit!* He thought, as he mused on his younger years that few females he encountered could handle a dick like this in the days before he was married.

He allowed her to continue on her own for a while before gripping her hair force-feeding her a little more of his dick. She gasped, but took it in stride trying to maintain the rhythm she had already established. With the next stroke, he forced a bit more down her throat, which brought tears to her eyes and came extremely close to stimulating her gag reflex. As the tears rolled down her face, he smiled down at her and then gave her the rest, holding her pinned balls deep for two to three seconds, an eternity to her, causing her to cough and almost gag once again before pulling her to her feet.

Releasing her hair, he told her to grab his neck. She obeyed him instinctively as he dipped slightly and gripped her thighs, lifting her onto his dick in one smooth motion. She held onto him while he fucked her in front of his desk. His strength amazed her because she was being flung up and down on his dick with minimal help from her, as she barely held on while being propelled along his thick shaft. He ensured her pussy traveled the full length of his dick on every stroke and she screamed in symphony every time her ass hit his pelvis, as her pussy took a pounding from a new angle.

She looked at the wall behind her as he fucked her displaying all of his career accomplishments and smiled inwardly thinking if she had her way a new plaque for good dick would sit next to the one for Company Grade Officer of the year. She heard her ass and thighs slap and her pussy juices splash every time he brought her down on his dick, until she felt the familiar sensation building up. Prior to this she had only felt that sensation with a mouth on her vagina doing wonderful circles around her clit with a tongue.

She squeezed him tightly exhaling, "I think I'm about to come," she whispered near his ear before screaming out and attempting to jump off his dick at the intensity of the feeling.

She felt steel in his hands. He gripped her hips tightly not allowing her to get down, and began to whine and grind out her pussy like most Trinidadian men are taught to do as a toddler before their first Carnival.

"Come girl," he whispered, as he continued to ream out her pussy with his hip movement making her pleasure hole spray out its juices with force while she cried out in ecstasy.

Feeling her shudders lessen, he carried her to the other side of his desk and laid her on top of it. He sat in his leather chair and adjusted the height and began to treat her pussy like the succulent dish it was. The sensation soothed, relieved, and thrilled her after the pounding she had just endured. His clean-shaven face dove deep between her legs and sucked her pussy while placing two long, strong fingers inside her to rub where some experts say the mysterious G-spot lurks.

"Aahh that feels so good!" she grinded as he continued to work lips, fingers and tongue as only an experienced practitioner could.

She couldn't believe her Commander was eating her pussy so well, as if she had taught him exactly how to do it. "OOhhh, go ahead Sir," she moaned, as she rubbed his smooth head. The pleasurable pressure began to build once again as she felt her pussy getting wetter and wetter, until he abruptly stopped and pulled her off the table. He spun her around and looped the leather belt around her neck before bending her face down once again onto the oak desk. He began to ram her from behind once more and she felt the constriction around her throat tighten as he continued pounding her more forcefully than he had before.

She was frightened a bit, but the way her body was responding to being choked and fucked at the same time amazed her. She felt herself close to blacking out as he had her legs pinned to the desk while he fucked her. With the belt wrapped around her neck he was pulling her torso off the desk with it as he continued to ram her pussy. She tried to gain some type of air to her lungs by trying to grab the belt. She saw stars as blackness began to close in on her consciousness when he suddenly released her, as her pussy sprayed again in the most powerful orgasmic climax that she had ever felt before in her entire life.

He continued to fuck her as Brooklyn, finally able to draw breath, screamed in orgasmic bliss. She heard him start to moan, feeling an increased steel in his dick just as he let out a primal grunt before pulling out his dick and spraying her ass and back with a hot load of jizz while stroking his dick to ensure a full burst.

"Your pum-pum sweet, you know gal," he smiled.

Spent and shuddering on the desk, Brooklyn remained silent thinking she now knew what people prone to addiction felt after that first hit. As she thought to herself, *Fuck my life!*

JOINT SPOUSE ENDEAVOURS

WARREN AND CORINNE MAZEK HAD been married for two years, but had only been living in the same house for about seven months. That timeframe coincided with them being on the same continent for more than thirty days. This was the longest time they had spent together since meeting three years ago on a deployment to Bahrain. Warren Mazek was a Petty Officer Second Class, and Corinne, formerly known as Corinne Tyler or CT, as Warren called her, was a Staff Sergeant in the Air Force. She was an enlisted intelligence analyst and he was a U.S Navy courier. Being married for two years, yet only living together for a short time was not their choice or design, but getting married to another member of the U.S. Armed Forces did not guarantee you got stationed in the same place. Things were especially difficult for members of different branches to get placed in the same vicinity, hence the 17 month wait in order to be able to live in the same house. They were now stationed at Royal Air Force Base Mildenhall in the United Kingdom. Warren grew up in San Francisco and had been in Jacksonville, Florida before being moved to England. He missed the sun tremendously. Corinne had been relocated from Mchord Air Base, in Washington State. A military brat used to constant moves, she felt right at home with the rain, dreariness, and long winter nights of England. The Mazeks were what you would call an eclectic mix. Warren, 5 feet and 7 inches tall, was of Filipino and Black descent. Stout and strong, he enjoyed moving around heavy plates in the gym. Corinne, 5 feet and 9 inches tall, was of white and Korean descent with long pretty legs that most women would die for. Some of her friends joked that she should insure her legs for a million apiece as Rhianna was rumored to have done. In addition to that, her full-sized C cups made every blouse she wore a spectacular event.

They met at the club on base in Bahrain during a Country and Western night, no less. Corinne and her friends were drinking whiskey sours and two-stepping, captivating the crowd's attention. The girls even put a few Texas and Tennessee boys to shame on the dance floor. Warren and some of the other Seamen were posted at the bar sharing a bottle of Jack Daniels, enjoying the sight of the dancing women. He didn't really care for country music, but he enjoyed seeing pretty women. The sight of the women was especially refreshing to him after his last mission. The past four days in and out of Iraq and Afghanistan, whilst sleeping in the cargo compartment of C-130s, was harrowing. The Jack Daniels and coke, combined with the dancing women, was a great reprieve to the dust, dryness, and squalor of Iraq and Afghanistan. The meeting between them didn't even occur in the club, it was afterwards in a somewhat unorthodox chain of events. There are no Waffle Houses or IHOPS in Bahrain. Therefore, the inebriated patrons have no options for food after a night out. Hence, when Warren's friend Cody overheard Corinne's friend Emma mention she would do strange things for some breakfast, he couldn't help but offer his cooking services along with an escort to the mess hall. Cody, Warren, Ayuhi and Aaron then proceeded to escort Corinne, Emma, Julie, Stacy and Katharrine to the mess hall. Cody had the key to the closed kitchen and proceeded to open up the place in order to misappropriate government supplies in the hopes of finding out what strange things Emma would be willing to do after being fed. Warren was an introvert and not prone to spontaneous conversations with strangers, nor was he searching for a new fishing hole so he kept his engagement with the ladies to a minimum. He kept to himself, allowing his more eager friends to seek recruitment from the women. In no time flat Cody had prepared enough bacon, sausage, grits, eggs and toast to feed all nine of them twice over. Warren sat at the table eating with everyone minus Cody, who was busy cleaning up the mess he made preparing the food, and Emma, who was keeping him company while he did it. Warren ate his food slowly, savoring everything after four days of MREs, while listening to Aaron and Ayuhi jockey for position, throwing out the base to see which of the four women left at the table would give back the mid-range. Aaron, a 6'1 195-pound red haired Caucasian guy from Ohio, and Ayuhi, a 6'4 235 pound Samoan, were bantering back and forth with Corinne and her friends, whilst Warren enjoyed Cody's handy work. She didn't even pay attention to Warren at first, even though they had all been introduced. She usually kept away from shorter men, and he was definitely not her type at first glance. It wasn't until Aaron and Ayuhi started to get a little rowdy trying to impress the women that she suddenly really looked at him for what he was. Ayuhi threw a salt shaker at Aaron. Preparing to retaliate, Aaron grabbed the saltshaker when Warren suddenly spoke without raising his voice.

"You two need to chill the fuck out. Cody works here, so stop ODing and show some respect." Aaron, salt shaker in hand, paused mid throw and put the salt back on the table.

"You right, dawg," they both said almost immediately. Corinne saw who the alpha male was in that sequence and was intrigued. She could tell what he said was not an attempt to impress or show off, just an obvious concern for a friend and a no-nonsense attitude. She would think about that night often during her married life, wondering if her pussy got wet due to his command of the other men or his concern for a friend. Corinne later discovered that his dick was also stout, barrel-like, and definitely commanded attention in any setting.

On a cold Friday evening in November, Corinne waited on Warren to come in from working a 12-hour shift. She had been an observer at the urinalysis center, so she had been looking at a plethora of pussies all day and was eager for Warren to get home so she could get hers eaten. She received a text from him letting her know he was on the way home.

She texted him back.

> Hurry up baby, I've seen a lot of vaginas today and need to see a dick soon!!

He replied almost immediately.

LOL! 20 minutes, CT, and I will be there to
put you back on the right track.

Within 18 minutes, Warren arrived inside their
Newmarket home to find Corinne as naked as the day
she was born, but with better attributes. She was sitting
on the couch with a thick towel underneath her as well
as a sheet under that. Corinne was a squirter. He paused
momentarily to admire her freshly shaved vagina with
the landing strip right above and smiled. "So, I don't get
to take a shower first, huh?"

Without replying, she gently patted her pussy while
shaking her head no.

"You 'bout that life, ain't you," he stated matter-of-
factly while dropping his bag down and taking off his hat.
Kneeling in front of his wife, he briefly thought about
removing his top knowing she would be spraying all over
him shortly. *Ahh, fuck it, it's laundry weekend anyway.* He
licked Corinne's pussy.

"Mmmhh. I have been waiting for this moment all
day," she whispered, engrossed in the feel of his tongue
as he relished her taste. Corinne rested her heels on his
shoulders as he licked from top shelf to bottom shelf.
Savoring her entire pussy, he lavished licks and sucks on
the lips below her waist and the surrounding area with
only momentary flicks of his tongue on her clitoris. He
wanted to build up her excitement and took his time to
do so. A bi-sexual ex-girlfriend once told him that when
eating pussy, taking the time to enjoy the full vagina
accoutrements is essential. Her lessons taught him not
just to suck on the clit, but to enjoy the entire area and

spend time with it like an old friend. Continuing to use his tongue, Corinne leaned her head back and reveled in the feel of the man she loved dining on her. Focused on her pink pearl, Warren knew she was about to spray him when she grabbed the back of his head with her heels still seated on his shoulders. A big wrestling fan growing up, he imagined himself in one of the Undertaker's signature moves, the Hell's Gate. Corinne pulled his head closer to her and squeezed her legs around his head as she came screaming and spraying her love juice all over him. Laughing as he caught his breath after Corinne's Undertaker impression, he stood up and kissed her before beginning to remove his top.

"What are you laughing at, Warren?" she said perplexed.

"I felt like I was in a Royal Rumble or steel cage match with the Undertaker just now. I know exactly what the hell's gate feels like," he laughed again.

"I can't believe you have a naked woman with a clean, freshly shaved puki in front of you and you're thinking about grown men rolling around on the floor with each other," she smiled as she put her feet together and stroked the bulge in his pants with her feet.

"Okay, smart-ass, I got your grown man right here." He moved her feet off him and took her hand, standing her up as he unbuckled his pants.

"By the way, I like the way you threw a little Filipino in there with your shaved puki." He kissed her before turning her around to plunge his barrel inside her. She was used to his girth, but it still made her breathe a little differently as she met his rhythm. Warren tried to punish her for the little joke she made, but he felt her meeting

74

his every stroke as she stood on her tiptoes and used her arms to propel herself back from the couch.

She turned around to smile at him, "You mad, baby?"

Warren just grunted and kept his stroke going.

"Put it in my ass, then," she taunted him.

He paused and then let a bomb of spit fall right on Corinne's asshole as he pulled his dick out of her pussy.

"Good aim, babe," she said while grabbing his slick member and steering it into her Top Shelf, as she liked to call it. The tightness of her asshole gripped his head as she tried to relax herself to let him in. She guided him in slowly as she shuddered, receiving his thickness. Even though it wasn't her first, time she still had to take a moment to get adjusted. With only the head inside her, she pulled him forward so she could get on her knees on the couch and then she allowed him to plunge it in all the way. Warren enjoyed the tightness and the heat as he slow stroked Corinne's top shelf. He knew how much she liked it, since she could orgasm anally without any clit stimulation. She whimpered as he built up speed and force, then he let another bomb of spit land on the shaft of his dick to keep her ass moisturized.

Warren knew she was about to come when she started opening and closing her hands repeatedly. Her familiar cry excited him and he sprayed inside her shortly after her pussy gave him another burst of love juices.

"Ooohh! Every time you fuck me it gets better. I like when I can get you mad; it makes your dick harder," she laughed.

"Whatever you say Corinne, my dick is plenty hard without you trying to tease me."

"Just sit down so I can take your boots and pants off and we can take a shower," she pushed him onto the couch.

After their shower, they sat in their matching Minions onesies watching Luke Cage on Netflix. Warren never got around to asking Corinne exactly what she was doing earlier, as he suddenly realized in her text message she said she had been looking at women's privates all day.

"Why were you looking at vaginas all day?"

"I got tagged for observer duty at the DDR."

"DDR?" He quizzed.

"The drug demand reduction center slash agency or whatever. I mean, I have enjoyed seeing a pussy or two before but this was a little out of hand. I never realized women's love boxes were as varied as their faces."

Her statement threw Warren off a little bit because he had never heard her talk about another woman like that before. The entire time they were together there was never a discussion about how many people they had been with before or any of that shit. They got tested for all diseases before tying the knot and that was enough for Warren. He learned by reading the Malcom X autobiography when he was a teen not to ask a woman a question about another man because, as his pops co-signed Malcolm in saying, *Ten times to one she is going to lie about it, and if she tells you the truth you'll probably realize you were better off not knowing in the first place.* All those lines ran through his head but he couldn't resist asking the obvious question.

"What do you mean, *enjoyed seeing a pussy or two before*?"

"Warren, it's 2016. I have been with a woman before, more than once."

An unfamiliar stillness filled the room as he processed the information while Bring The Ruckus from Wu-Tang played in the background and Luke Cage whipped some ass on the TV screen. He was a little flabbergasted, but managed to smile after his momentary silence.

"Okay, then," he chuckled at himself for being a little confused. Corinne turned his head towards her and kissed him gently.

"You are such a prude, but that's why I love you." She traced her fingers down from his face over his broad chest and gripped his balls before kissing his cheek and whispering in his ear, "Let's go to Innocence tomorrow night. It's a Hustle event and I'll pull something for us to bring home. You can watch me get my pussy eaten. I might let you fuck her too, if you behave and fuck me right now."

She squeezed his balls a little harder and felt the bulge grow in his onesie. They would have to watch Episode 4 of Luke Cage another day as they left the couch and went into the bedroom. Saturday night came fast and Warren was a little apprehensive about the events to come. His history with women was extensive but he was more of a traditionalist than he thought. As a teen he had seen various pornos and entertained the thought of being with more than one woman at a time, but the opportunity never presented itself to him before this. It didn't help that Corinne had been teasing him all day and asking him if he was scared. She was poking so much he almost wanted to stay home but he wasn't going to miss this.

"You better not embarrass me either, Warren, because whoever we bring back home is going to know how good

you are by what I say so you better not come all quick."
She walked by him giggling after she threw that one
at him.

"Way to support your husband's success, smart-ass."

He smacked her ass before she could get out of
his reach. They took a cab and got to the club around
ten-thirty since they were not planning on staying until
closing. March Madness by Future was banging out when
Warren made it to the bar and bought a double shot of
Amaretto Ciroc and pineapple juice for himself, and a
glass of white Cabernet for Corinne. She stuck her tongue
out at him as she danced in front of him suggestively. He
admired how she looked in her full-length dress with a
slit that went clear up to the top of her thigh. The orange
dress clung to her skin above the waist and the deep
cleavage displayed her best feature in excellent fashion.
He smiled as he sipped his drink, thinking of how lucky
he was to find this woman with such a free spirit who he
knew loved him unconditionally. Corinne didn't have any
panties on and he shifted his dick to the other side of his
boxer briefs knowing she would get him hard. He wanted
his dick pointed up when the inevitable happened and he
got aroused. She smiled, watching him adjust his package,
and came close.

"What are you moving around in there, sir? Did
you come already?" She kissed him on the cheek and
giggled. Warren just shook his head while smiling and
took another sip of his drink. He knew not to battle wits
with Corinne and her quick tongue. As the club filled to
capacity, Warren leaned against the wall in the back of
the club near the exit to the smoke area while Corinne

danced within his sight. He watched as both men and women walked by checking her out, but it didn't faze him. He knew who she was going home with and never felt threatened by any of that. Corinne could handle herself anyway, and none of the guys who tried to dance with her got out of hand when she turned them away, so he didn't have to move. She was dancing and talking to some of her friends when she suddenly turned back to look at him, letting him know that she was going to the dance floor with her friends. He nodded his head in acknowledgment and watched her disappear into the crowd. Scanning the area while bopping his head to the music, Warren continued to nurse his drink enjoying the sight of the different asses walking to and fro. Ooouuu by Young M.A. came on and the crowd noise rose to a higher pitch as everyone acknowledged their love for the song in unison. A thick, light skinned woman with big frizzy hair walked by Warren when the hook came on as if it was her theme music. *Ooouuu indeed!* he thought, as he looked at her ass while she walked by him. He wondered if she had on super tight jeans but realized they were actually tights when she stopped a few feet in front of him. Sipping on a Kopparberg cider, she rocked her hips back and forth while Warren appreciated the sight. His older brother would have called her a Triple H, which was an ode to a Black Sheep skit he used to recite when Warren was a kid. Triple H turned around and looked at Warren for a few seconds and their eyes met. He smiled and lifted his drink as if to say cheers, she smiled and turned back around. Corinne came back with her friends' minutes after that exchange and leaned against Warren and began to grind her ass on him. Warren enjoyed the grind as he slipped his hand in the slit on Corinne's dress and squeezed her thigh. Triple H turned around again and saw Corinne grinding on him and smiled. She raised her drink to him as he had done to her earlier.

Corinne leaned back, "Did you make a friend?"

"Naw, that's just Triple H."

"Triple H?" She scrunched her face up.

"I don't know her. I'm just fucking with you. She's just showing a little love, that's all."

"Is that the one, baby? I think you like that behind of hers," she giggled.

"That is true, but I love yours. It's different." They both laughed at that, then Corinne stopped grinding and walked over to Triple H. Warren watched as she put her hands around the other woman's waist and whispered something in her ear before walking her to the dance floor. All he could do is just shake his head and smile at his woman's moxie. They were gone for about five or six songs when he saw Corinne leading Triple H by the hand back to where he was standing.

"Warren, I told her what you called her so she agreed to let me introduce her as such. This is Triple H. Triple H, this is my husband Warren."

"Whatever happened to no snitching, CT? I thought you were on my team." They all laughed as Triple H and Warren shook hands.

"My wife is a little wild, so you can tell me your real name, I feel like a jerk calling you Triple H now."

"I think you have to earn it so Triple H will be my

name until you prove what your wife told me on the dance floor."

She smiled while looking him up and down before Corinne grabbed her waist again and began dancing right in front of him. Corinne kissed her while still dancing, and Warren felt the barrel begin to grow as he fought to keep it under control. Corinne backed up against him and pulled Triple H with her. She grabbed his hand and slid it under her dress and inside her core, already wet with excitement. She let Warren caress it before pulling his hand out to suck his fingers and then kissed Triple H again. Corinne grabbed them both by the hand after that and led them to the exit. Warren smiled as he saw a dude he recognized from the gym give him the nod of approval. The cab ride was a blur as Warren let the girls do their thing, trying to keep himself from getting too excited and stay on an even keel. It didn't help that, while the women kissed, Triple H reached back and stroked his dick through his jeans. Inside the house Corinne undressed Triple H and led her into the large multi-headed shower. He just watched them go as his inexperience kept him seated on the couch. He heard the women laughing a few seconds before they both called out in a singsong voice. "Hey Warren, come and shower with us, don't be scared."

CT's smartass strikes again, he thought while undressing and heading to the shower. He paused for a second before closing the door in appreciation of the two beautiful women soaping each other. As he entered, Corinne kissed him and began to soap him up and Triple H followed suit.

"You gave a nice description; it is like a nice barrel,"

Triple H smiled at Corinne while soaping Warren's dick at the same time.

"Wait until you feel it inside you," Corinne squeezed Warren's ass and kissed him again. He grabbed their asses as he swapped kisses between women. Each of their hands held his dick moving up and down in tandem. Corinne disengaged herself to grab the soap and wash rag. Kneeling, she cleaned Triple H's pussy as she continued to kiss Warren and stroke his barrel. She knew Warren loved to eat clean, so she took great care in preparing it for him. Taking one of the shower heads off the wall, Corinne rinsed the soap from Triple H's crotch and soaped her own hand up before slipping a finger in Triple H's top shelf. Triple H moaned but didn't push Corinne away. Corinne played with Triple H's clit while slipping her soapy middle finger in and out of the other woman's top shelf. Triple H responded by grinding on the finger in her ass and biting on Warren's lip a little, which made him open his eyes and back away, seeing what his wife was doing. Triple H used her grip on Warren's dick to steer him downward. He began to eat her pussy while his wife continued her top shelf action while gripping Triple H's breasts and pinching her nipples at the same time. Triple H orgasmed with a yell and nearly toppled them all in the shower as her legs buckled briefly.

"You two are mean, double teaming me like that," she complained sarcastically in her British accent.

"I'll let Warren show you what mean really is, if you two can take me to ecstasy without taking *Ecstasy*," said Corinne. The trio cleaned each other up again before strolling into the bedroom. Warren grabbed Corinne and wanted to eat her pussy but she stopped him and nodded her head towards Triple H.

"Let her try. I want to see what she can do, and I want you to watch." Triple H smiled and kissed Warren as he stood up from his position.

"Enjoy the show big boy. We'll get to you soon enough." Triple H squatted and swallowed the head of the barrel to suck briefly before focusing her mouth on Corinne's waiting pussy. Warren stood at the edge of the bed and watched as his wife wrapped her hands around Triple H's long hair. Her familiar moan sound filled the air as Triple H worked her magic. Corinne's hand began to open and close rapidly as she started her build up to peak excitement levels. Corinne came hard and Warren felt his dick leaking when she screamed out.

"Look at him girl, I think he may be too excited," Triple H smiled.

"Don't worry about my husband, he is not a minute man."

"I hope so, Corinne."

"Shit, me too," Warren said. Both women laughed at that and pulled him onto the bed.

"Guests suck first," Corinne mini-bowed to Triple H. Licking the cum off his dick, Triple H spit in her hands and began to suck his thick shaft while circling the head of his barrel with her hand. He pulled Corinne up to sit astride his face and sucked on her clit as Triple H stopped sucking his shaft and attempted to get the head of the barrel as far up her throat as she could. Triple H was an expert with the suction and she slurped and sucked his dick until he lost concentration while sucking on Corinne. Warren fiercely squeezed his wife's ass as he exploded in Triple H's mouth.

"Good stuff girl, but that's not all my guy has. Hop on that dick if you can handle it."

"You're a cheeky one, aren't you?" Triple H replied as she accepted the challenge. Warren's dick was unusual for Triple H. She had experienced longer in the past but she couldn't remember anyone thicker. She sat cautiously as the barrel filled her womb while keeping her hand on his chest and leg to avoid screaming. Corinne, eager to watch Warren go to work, stopped riding his face and turned around to watch the show. Triple H, finally accommodating herself on the barrel, began to grind back and forth. Moaning and gripping her breasts she enjoyed being spread wide. She did this for this for five to ten minutes while Corinne watched, playing with herself.

Triple H looked at Corinne and said "You like the way I'm fucking your husband?"

The question must have struck a nerve, or maybe it was the look in her eyes when she said it, but Corinne suddenly grabbed her by the hair and pulled her off Warren.

"Baby, please fuck the dog shit out of this girl for me." Warren obliged by pulling the other woman to the edge of the bed and threw her legs over his shoulders burying the barrel as deep as he could. Triple H screamed and tried to back away but Warren was too strong and Corinne aided in the punishment by holding her shoulders while Warren pounded her. Corinne leaned down and licked her ear as Triple H whimpered at the pounding.

"I told you I would show you mean." Triple H's legs began to shake involuntarily as she neared orgasm again.

Her pussy gripped his dick as she came and screamed out while Corinne covered her mouth to muffle the sound staring into her husband's eyes as he neared his second explosion.

"Fuck my mouth, baby," Corinne begged. Warren pulled out of Triple H as she curled up in the after throes of her punishing orgasm and Corinne jumped right in to take him in her mouth.

"Yeah, CT," he exhaled deeply as she sucked and stroked his dick with both hands. She spun her tongue around his dick and sucked until he burst in her mouth with the sweet taste she loved.

"Mmmmmhh," she continued to suck, draining him of strength. Warren eased his wife off his dick and sat next to her on the bed, putting his arm around her.

"Damn CT, this was nice. Very fun."

"No problem, babe. Didn't I tell you when we met I would expand your mind to new things?" She giggled.

"You are such a smart ass," Warren removed his arm. Triple H, now recovered, chimed in, "She is a cheeky one."

They both looked back at her and laughed.

"Sorry for the pounding I gave a little while ago, but we work together in this house as you can see."

"No problem, Warren. It was painful but good. By the way, it's Amanda."

"Amanda?" He was confused.

"My real name is Amanda."

"Ahh, nice to meet you Amanda." They shook hands again and were joined by Corinne laughing at the irony.

ABOUT THE AUTHOR

Marlo Delano Maitland is a twenty-two-year Air Force veteran who has served his country in over nineteen countries. His rich and varied experiences have led him to create a compilation of fictional stories based on the lives of some of the many people he has encountered over the years. Working with all services during his tenure, he saw the undisputable truth of all human beings in their need for sexual satisfaction. Be it same-sex or heterosexual, physical needs abound and they will be met regardless of rules or circumstance. The single father of three from Brooklyn, New York enjoys reading, writing and rooting for his beloved Jets and Knicks to no avail. You can often catch him cussing at the TV on any given Sunday when the Jets are playing, or when the Knicks make a cameo on primetime TV to be whipped by the opposing team. In his opinion, they are not worth paying for NBA league pass. You can share your own Classified Encounters with him at marlomaitland@classifiedencounters.net. If you're lucky some of your stories will be shared in the next volume.